CONVERSATIONS WITH A WILD MAN

R. E. DANIELS

outskirts
press

Outskirts Press, Inc.
http://www.outskirtspress.com

ISBN: 978-1-4787-9517-9

Outskirts Press and the "OP" logo are trademarks belonging to Outskirts Press, Inc.

PRINTED IN THE UNITED STATES OF AMERICA

Dedicated to:

Boise Gilkison, who had the courage to embrace the wild man, which gave me permission to do the same. In spite of the world's attempt at diminishing your joyful noise, it has been heard and is a cherished reminder that carried me throughout my life. You are dearly loved.

Duane Pearson, who freely offered a wild man his intellect, and inspired the exponential growth within me. You are deeply respected as a father, and the dearest friend.

To Kyle Ann Daniels, who chose to love a wild man unconditionally, and gave from every part of herself to show me it was possible. You are, above all, my greatest treasure.

And

To Mike Thomas, who taught me that loving what I do isn't about what I do...it is about how I love. As everyone in Oz knows, even the greatest courage, intellect, and heart will go unjustified without some great and powerful wizard to pull it together and give it direction. I will never be able to express my gratitude.

CONTENTS

WARNING

Before continuing with this endeavor, there are some things that must be clearly understood. I am not a politician. I am not a theologian. I am not a behavioral scientist of any sort. I am not, by any traditional definition, a minister, rabbi, counselor, priest, or pastor. I realize that there are many things I am not, but I feel it necessary to make it understood that I am not any of these things.

What I am is a professional investigator. I investigate the failures that occur to equipment typically found in large, industrial settings. The broken equipment under investigation is nearly always critical to the overall productivity of the facility in which it is installed. For example, a large generator experiences a catastrophic failure in a power plant. This normally means that it will cost several million dollars to repair, and tens of millions in interrupted business because the facility is unable to produce electricity for the duration of time those repairs are implemented.

The purpose of any investigation undertaken is to determine the exact cause of the failure, whether it was a poorly fabricated component, inadequate maintenance, improper use, or insufficient overall design. Once I have identified the root cause of the equipment failure, my task is completed. I leave it up to underwriters, adjusters, lawyers, and anyone else involved to determine who is responsible for paying those bills. Although it may seem callous, I cannot care who pays the bills for such an occurrence.

It has to be that way. A dear friend and colleague of mine told me that the only thing we have of any value in this business is our integrity. Without integrity, we are no better than any opinion that can be bought for cash and supported by bull. Professionally, I must forge through each day with an unwavering pursuit of the truth regardless of the consequences.

With tens and often hundreds of millions of dollars at stake, it can be imagined how carefully the results of each investigation are scrutinized, so everything I report must make sense to me and whoever reads it. It can also be imagined how, for every person who appreciates my efforts, there are at least as many who do not.

As with any occupation, there are certain skill sets that must be acquired to perform the task. This particular occupation typically requires many years of training and experience accompanied by certain character traits, such as the aforementioned integrity. Thick skin and an unquenchable curiosity may be other beneficial character traits. There may be many desirable educational, experiential, and behavioral attributes, and in any measure or combination, that would well serve a professional investigator, but the one thing that has served me above all others is common sense.

My occupation has afforded me the opportunity to travel the world and have fascinating conversations with incredible people from all walks of life. These conversations have encompassed professional goals, politics, religion, family, personal relationships, spirituality, and everything else under the sun. Through the course of these conversations over these many years, I have applied the skill sets I have acquired in pursuit of the truth, attempting to find the common sense where none seems to exist, in the areas of our lives that bring meaning to it. My father once said to me, "I stopped one day and looked at the world and couldn't make any sense of what was going on. Makes me wonder why they call such a rarity *common sense*."

It is not my function to alter anyone's perspective, but simply offer my own. It is not my purpose to administer the consequences of learning any truth, simply to find it. I am not a politician. I am not a theologian. I am not a behavioral scientist of any sort. I am not, by any traditional definition, a minister, rabbi, counselor, priest, or pastor. I am, however, certain that for everyone who reads this, there will be those who appreciate what has been found, and at least as many who will not.

I'm just a guy with unusually thick skin. Fair warning has been given.

PROLOGUE: THE WAKE-UP CALL

God wakes me up every morning, usually around 4:00 AM, and usually with the malicious memory I made of some particular event exemplifying chunks of wasted life. Drugs, women, alcohol, violence; they're all there, and they all show up randomly rotating their wake-up responsibilities at roughly 4:00 AM.

Then, I usually hear Him thundering down the marble corridor, and just as the door slams open, He snatches a garbage can full of discarded creativity and screams, "GET OUT OF THAT RACK!"

The can reaches the top of its arch, and noticeably pauses before rattling to the polished tile floor, splashing creativity all over everything. "I SAID, GET OUTTA THAT RACK!!" He bellows. Then adds, "AND CLEAN THIS PLACE UP!"

I don't get too excited anymore, or take it too personally. God usually wakes me up in this manner. I lie there and crack open one eye and find myself staring immediately into the snoring face of Motivation. I almost always cuff him hard on the head asking, "What the hell are you good for?" He rarely answers. Instead, he resigns himself to farting loudly and rolling over, taking all the covers with him, knowing perfectly well that if his gastric habits don't drive me out of bed, the lack of covers will. It's always a little disheartening that this is the lazy bastard's best effort for getting me to crawl out of bed.

With nothing to look at but his hairy, sweating back, I roll over to find Imagination. Her breath usually reeks of one too many lies the night before. Because of her hangover, she, as well, sleeps like the dead through all the commotion. The glaring, naked bulbs flash on overhead and I close my eyes tightly, throwing my hands over my face.

The whole time, God is rattling a nightstick across the rails on the foot of the bed and still screaming with a voice like sand grinding between my fillings. Although I can't imagine it possible, He manages to scream even louder, and now He's pounding the nightstick on the metal bed frame to enunciate His words. "I'M TELLIN' YOU FOR THE LAST TIME TO **GET! (CLANG!) OUT! (CLANG!) AH-THAT! (CLANG!) RACK! (CLANG!)**"

"Shut up," I cough feebly. "Just give me five more minutes." I manage to open my eyes momentarily as I beg. It almost always scares me when I open my eyes for the morning focus. His face is right in front of me and His nose is almost touching mine, and I can tell by the look of utter rage smeared across His face that I'm not going to get my extra five minutes. "Aw'right," I cough again. "I'm up."

I shove Motivation off the edge of the bed and onto his fat ass. "You're kind of a worthless bastard," I state bluntly, as the blankets and pillows follow him to the floor.

I look over my shoulder. Imagination is lying there, face up, perfectly still. I've got several choice words for her as well, but pity gets the better of me, and I check her pulse instead. As I collect one of the blankets and throw it over her, I listen to her weak, shallow panting and wonder, "Where on earth *were* you last night?"

"RIGHT NOW!" The whole room shudders under God's command.

"Yeah. I hear ya. Ya don't have to scream, ya know." I'm up and idling toward the head by then. After years of being roused this way, you might think that I'd be used to it. But invariably, on my way to the bathroom, I nearly break my neck slipping in the creativity that was thrown all over the place earlier. "I'm not cleaning that shit up either!" I yell over my shoulder, trying to shake the ooze off my bare foot.

Until now, that was just how I started the day. I always figured that God was just not a morning person. Or, perhaps, He felt that, since He didn't get to sleep in, there was no reason to let me. I naturally assumed everyone started the day in pretty much the same fashion: nightsticks, garbage cans, and plenty of hollering, with, of course, varying degrees of intensity, but all by a relatively similar process.

But this morning was miraculously different. At exactly 3:53 AM, I was gently guided out of sleep and into a state of full alertness with a memory that was given to me, and not one that I made. The memory itself seemed so simple as to be comical. It was of nothing more than sitting and having a conversation with a friend.

In the discussion we had covered every topic available and the talk ranged from easy to excited; impactful to lighthearted. Attention never diminished, enthusiasm never waned, and vanity never donned. It was a memory of two people just talking, and it was majestic.

On this morning, I sensed the jasmine breath of God behind my ear whispering, "Good morning."

I could smell pastries baking and freshly ground coffee percolating and thought, *Yum.* I felt Imagination slip her slender arm over my waist as she tilted her head and gently kissed me on the throat. She pulled herself closer, nuzzling her nose into the side of my neck, and the rhythm of her heart and warmth of her breath was sweet as we lay in the darkness.

God drifted up, eased onto the edge of the bed, and softly ran His fingers through my hair. "Do you want me to come back later?" He asked. And although He barely made a sound, I could feel the clarity of His voice vibrating through me.

Maybe just five more minutes, I thought, without opening my eyes.

"Take as long as you want," He whispered. "Motivation already has a fresh batch of creativity baking and the insight is brewing, so there's no need to hurry." He padded across the glistening tile floor, paused at the door, and looking back over His shoulder, sang, "I'll turn on the lights when you're ready. Did you like the memory this morning?"

"It was beautiful. Thank you so much," I gushed, still not opening my eyes.

And then, for no apparent reason, He said, "I love you, young man."

The smell of coffee, and now fresh bread, the warmth of Imagination holding me, the memory of a friendly conversation, and the quiet bumping and thumping of God getting ready for work was exactly comfortable. I turned over, kissed Imagination between the eyebrows, and sat up. "Where are you going?" she asked sleepily.

"I'm not sure," I told her, "but I can't wait to get started." As I thought about the taste of fresh creativity dunked in insight, it occurred to me at just that moment that I was joyful...and I wondered if anyone else in the world ever got to wake up like this.

1

I'LL SEND, NOT ONE, BUT THREE

I.

At well over forty years old now, Cowboy could scarcely believe it, but it was true. It began when he was a skinny, long-legged six-year-old boy wearing hand-me-downs from his two older brothers and a brand-new red cowboy hat he got for his birthday. It was the Red Ryder hat with the white latigo sewn all the way around the brim, and the twisted cord strap that could be tightened to his chin with a wooden slide bead on windy days. He loved that hat. It was how he acquired the handle "Cowboy," which stuck to him the rest of his life.

He was living the American reality. He didn't know what the American dream was. He was, in fact, so far removed from the American dream that not only did he not know what it was, he hadn't ever met anyone who did. It wasn't surprising, really, since, at six years old, he hadn't met that many people.

On his first day of first grade, he met a nice kid garbed in similar attire who went by the name of Krank.

"Krank," he announced to Cowboy, "means *sick* in German."

"Cool!" Cowboy admired.

"What does Daniels mean?" Gary inquired of him the day they met.

For the life of him, Cowboy had no idea that a name could actually mean something. Mrs. Piana had been crossing the playground in front of them at that moment, carrying her black poodle tucked neatly under her arm like a football. Cowboy had heard that she was a member of some society in Europe or Spain or some other exotic island, and figured her name meant something very special, like "musical." He was even sure her dog's name probably meant something, betting on French for "something to step on."

Cowboy panicked. "Dog," he announced, that being the first thing that popped into his head. "It's Irish and it means dog," he reiterated with conviction, because even a six-year-old knows that when you lie, you're much more likely to get away with it if you do it with conviction.

"Really? Cool!" Gary admired right back.

Once discovering their names had meanings, and the commonalities they shared with unwavering courage and superior intellect, the two found themselves in the friend business. Their walkie-talkies buzzed long after dark during their backyard camping nights, blaring with crime-fighting missions and secret identities.

"Dog-one, Dog-one. This is Sick-one. Do you copy, over?"

"I copy, Sick-one, over," came young Cowboy's reply.

"I've got a disturbance at Mr. Day's residence. It looks like Ray Street's dog is attempting to break and enter the Days' rabbit cages. Do you copy, over?" Gary's voice crackled from the speaker.

"I copy, Sick-one. I'm gathering ammunition and heading your direction." At which point young Cowboy would fill his pockets with throwing gravel, pounce on his Stingray bicycle, and start pumping it to the other side of the neighborhood.

And so the school year went. The two young boys were nearly joined at the hip; a pair of jokesters who found endless sources of trouble and enjoyment by playing every prank two six-year-old minds could conceive of on a large allotment of siblings, as each had been blessed with four.

And so their school year continued, at least until the forces of evil combined and the death threats forced them to divert their attention to more destructive activities. Their deductive abilities left little doubt when identifying the perpetrators of such heinous acts. These letters warning them of their eminent doom were usually written with words clipped out of magazines or newspapers, and pasted on typing paper.

Their ingenious little minds concluded that Gary's older sister, who used only pink paste in school, was undoubtedly the source of those threats that used pink paste to adhere the clipped words to the typing paper.

"Brilliant deduction, Dog!"

"Elementary, my dear Sick!" was young Cowboy's reply.

Cowboy's twin sister always sent the death threats that smelled of lilac perfume because she fancied Gary a little. Cowboy's older brother always used clippings from the *News Letter Journal*, and Gary's younger sister always clipped from *The Star*. They were convinced that Sherlock Holmes had nothing on them.

One particularly well-trimmed letter—assembled with what Gary had determined to be Elmer's glue by its taste (for reasons that remained unknown to Cowboy, Gary liked to eat paste)— had them both befuddled. It was discovered during a bathroom break that the letters were trimmed out of a woodworking magazine and it was laced with words that neither of them could define.

It found them wandering into the unfinished basement of Cowboy's house searching for his father, who was busily gluing the leg back on the chair that the two boys had used for their previous prank.

"Take a look at this, Dad," Cowboy insisted and poked the page under his father's nose.

"WOOO. This one looks pretty serious." He looked the note up and down. "It's even got cuss words in it."

"What d'ya think we should do with it, Mr. Daniels?" Gary asked through a smile.

"I suggest you little bastards follow its advice and stay the hell outta my toolbox" was his barking response as he tossed the note back at them. He was a great kidder, although Gary seemed to lose his smile very quickly.

The last death threat managed to divert the boys' attention toward inventing. Their inventions were marvelously convincing, and each of them knew that Thomas Edison had nothing on them. These creations had the power to do so many things at once: cause instantaneous household pandemonium; grip their mothers in absolute terror; startle their fathers into vocal fits of abundant descriptiveness; and often mutilate the two young boys. They had the best scar collection in the entire school.

As their school year dwindled, the two suffered escalating panic, fearing they would not get to see each other at all during the summer vacation. Gary, who happened to be the smarter of the two, spawned the most brilliant idea; his mother could pick up his young friend for church on Sunday.

The depth of his genius was truly quite remarkable, since a parent would never let a child miss the opportunity to attend church, particularly if they themselves did not have to bear the burden of attendance. His plan was to have his best friend Cowboy sleep over every Saturday, and he could then be delivered home Sunday after church. Utterly brilliant to give them an idea that could not be refused by either Christian or agnostic.

Now, Cowboy loved his father, but even in his brief six years, he had a feeling that he may not be terribly missed during summer weekends. The young boy's American reality included a very large, very drunken, and very abusive father. He had once overheard his grandmother offer "womanizing, raging, wife-beating alcoholic" as a fairly accurate summation of his father.

Cowboy knew nothing of such things at six years old, but there always seemed to be what he described as "loud problems" at his house. His mother fell down a lot and was always taking pain pills and tranquilizers. Now at six years old, Cowboy couldn't be expected to know anything about drug addictions. He and Gary figured that if it couldn't be doctored with black tape and Vick's VapoRub, it was incurable.

With all of the problems getting louder and louder, Cowboy's parents agreed to permit him to stay Saturdays with the Kranks and be back home after church on Sundays. Although Gary's mother, Bethany, was notably shaken at the proposition, her Christianity won out and she agreed. The boys could not understand Bethany's hesitation until one Saturday evening while giggling their way through the underwear section of the Montgomery Ward's catalogue. There they discovered several words and letters neatly snipped from the title pages.

In the end, Bethany concluded that she must agree to take these boys to church, and if it came to pass that she ended up killing the little lunatics, well, at least they'd go to heaven. "A little God might do them boys a world of good," she said to herself.

Cowboy wasn't even convinced he knew what church was, but he knew it offered some brief respite from the loud problems and an entire congregation of new opportunities for the two pranksters. They attended the Baptist church, and as a six-year-old, Cowboy wouldn't know the difference between a Baptist and a titmouse.

One particular sermon from the "fire and brimstone" preacher caught his attention, and may have been the only one he had actually heard all summer. Bethany ushered Cowboy and Gary, Gary's four siblings, with Gary's stepfather in tow, to the very front pew, convincing herself that sitting there would keep them boys lined out and her husband awake. Neither worked.

The preacher stood before them, all sweaty and loud, throwing his arms about and yelling, "Ask and ye shall receive!" Continuing into screaming orations about asking straight from your heart, the blessings of God are plentiful, simply ask, and on and on and on, bellowing for what seemed to the boys to be eons, until the point in the sermon when everyone said "Amen."

"Finally!" was the word that caught in the back of Cowboy's throat. He didn't know much about church, or even what "amen" meant, except that it was time for ice cream. As Bethany's crew departed the church, the minister shook hands with parishioners, thanking them for coming, commenting on how hot it was, inviting them to come again, and so on and so on and so on. As they padded through the two large front doors, the preacher looked down at Gary and gently squeezed him on the shoulder.

"Did you boys listen to the sermon today?" he asked. But the manner in which he spoke convinced Cowboy that the preacher was from another planet: "D'joo boyz lizzen to da soymen t'day?" Bethany informed Cowboy when he asked later that the reverend was from some place called The South.

"Yes sir," Gary automatically spouted.

"Yes sir," Cowboy followed suit and straightened his spine a little.

"Well, den. What waz id about?" he asked, looking directly into Cowboy's eyes as if he'd just discovered who put the tack in his chair near the podium.

Gary nudged Cowboy while loosening the top button of his shirt. He was suddenly feeling very warm. "It was about asking God for stuff" was all Cowboy could say, since it was all he could remember.

"An' wood joo git it?" He continued his inquisition.

"Yes sir, if you asked for it right," Cowboy answered, brimming with confidence. Even he knew that grown-ups never had time for a third question.

"Datz a fine boy ya got dare, Mizzuz Krank," the preacher complimented.

"Yes, he is," she said proudly, smiling down at Cowboy, and immediately went to scowling at Gary.

Cowboy got extra ice cream at the Howdy Do Drive-In that bright Sunday morning. With Bud snoring loudly in the passenger seat, Bethany and her five children rattled Cowboy home in an old black station wagon, and dropping him off beside his house, waved good-bye, yelling, "See you Saturday, Cowboy" over her left shoulder. Cowboy nodded the brim of his Red Ryder hat in agreement and dashed to his room.

That evening found him with his brothers and sisters and mother sitting in front of an old black-and-white console television set watching *I Dream of Genie*. His twin sister was particularly fond of that show. She loved to watch Major Nelson get whatever he wanted with a nod and a blink from his genie. Then *Bewitched* came on with Darrin getting whatever he wanted with a little nose twitching from his wife. Sissy just loved the way Esmerelda always spoke in rhymes.

Then his father came home and some really loud problems started. Cowboy took Sissy by the hand and led her up the stairs where they could play in his room. She was prone to vertigo, so someone almost always had to hold her hand on the stairs. They sat playing on the floor, trying not to listen to so many problems causing so much crashing and yelling downstairs.

"What did you do in church today?" she asked her brother.

"We talked about God giving us what we wanted," Cowboy answered.

"Cool! He can do that?"

"Well, that's what the preacher said. He has bad breath," Cowboy added. Something broke downstairs; something glass. "It's probably time to go to bed," he told her.

"Can I sleep in here with you again?" she pleaded.

"Yeah, if you don't tell anyone." It wouldn't do well for a genius, crime-fighting inventor to be found allowing his sister to sleep in the bed with him.

"I won't," she promised.

They read *Three Blind Mice* because Sissy loved to hear the rhyming. They piled into the twin bed with her against the wall and pulled one of their grandmother's quilts up over their heads. They stayed there forever, listening to the problems continue downstairs. Somehow, Sissy managed to fall asleep.

Cowboy decided it was time to take the church thing for a test run. He softly slid out of bed and, kneeling at the edge, raised his hands together, sticking his index fingers directly under his chin. "God? I want my wishes to come true. I also want someone to come and make all the problems go away." Cowboy had said it so matter-of-factly that he was a bit surprised at how simple it all seemed. He didn't buy into it much, kneeling there, the whole time wondering why everyone didn't do it if it was so easy.

He didn't notice his sister sitting up. Her eyes were cracked open and looking directly at Cowboy. She rolled on her hip and, reaching her left hand toward the boy, pinched his right earlobe between her thumb and forefinger, and as plainly and clearly as any grown-up said, "So you know it's Me, I'll send, not one, but three." Then she started blinking furiously and trying desperately to twitch her nose.

"What are you doing?" Cowboy asked, trying to subdue his anxiety.

"Soup and...EWWW!" was all she said, and dropped her head back to her pillow.

Cowboy knew she was prone to talking in her sleep, since they had spent more time sleeping together than not those days, but he had never heard her do it with such clarity. *Oh well,* he thought, and wished his parents would "tone it down" as his father would say. *Sissy's going to wake up.* For lack of anything better to do, he crawled back into bed and pulled the quilt up to his chin. Before dozing off, he noticed that all the problems downstairs had somehow become quiet ones.

II. Free His Soul

Although he didn't know what one was, Cowboy awoke in the morning feeling as if he had a hangover. His stomach ached and his head hurt and his eyes didn't open all the way. He stumbled into the kitchen, where his mother was perched at the end of the table in her robe, smoking a Raleigh Filter. She told him that his hay fever was bothering him again, and rubbed Vicks all over his chest. Her eye was all purple and swollen.

"What happened to your eye? Gross!"

"I fell," she answered softly.

From the half-opened kitchen window, Cowboy heard the most wonderful sound on the planet. A coughing, rattling black station wagon, with a sheet of cardboard for a rear passenger window and a cracked windshield, clattered into the driveway. Gary came bouncing out, yelling for Cowboy.

"C'mon, Cowboy! C'mon! Uncle Boise's in town out at Grampa's house!" he yelled. "C'mon! Ya gotta meet Uncle Boise!" Gary was very excited.

"Mom?" he asked.

"How's your hay fever?"

"Great! I feel dine and fandy." Cowboy grinned at her. She returned a slight smile at his mixing up the words. It was a game the two of them would sometimes play.

"Okay." She nodded at the boy and yelled, "When are you coming home?" at his back dashing out the door.

"Later," Cowboy hollered over his shoulder and dove into the old station wagon.

Boise was Bethany's younger brother, and as they prattled through town, Gary was poking Cowboy and nudging him and loudly talking a hundred miles an hour.

"Uncle Boise is in the Army and he's home on leave and we're going fishing and he's been to Germany and he's tougher than both of your brothers put together and..." He paused. "YOU STINK!" His top lip sneered, making his nose wrinkle. "You smell like Vicks."

"Mom puts it on me sometimes 'cause I'm allergic to hay."

"I think you mean hay fever," Bethany corrected.

Before they knew it, they were pulling in to Gary's grandfather's driveway. Gary was hanging out the window and yelling.

"There he is! Uncle Boise! Uncle Boise!"

Cowboy couldn't see anything, being seated next to the cardboard window, but when the car finally came to a dusty stop, Cowboy slipped out the door and there in the drive stood a man: overly tall, overly thin, with broad shoulders, short brown hair, and a very clean-shaven face. Gary bolted across the dirt drive, diving at the man and screaming, "WOOHOO!"

Boise caught him as easily as a beach ball, pulled him against his chest, and vigorously scrubbed his hair. "Wat-er ya doin', ya little fish killer?"

Cowboy eased up a little closer, stunned at just how tall that fellow was, and got within five feet before being noticed. Boise gently set Gary back down on the dirt and looked over at Cowboy. He looked him all over and, though his grin didn't fade, it dimmed slightly. Cowboy could tell that Boise was thinking. The morning sun was behind Boise's shoulders, and Cowboy thought his neck would start hurting from looking up so high just to see this man's face. Cowboy didn't know it then, and was certain Boise didn't either, but in that blink of time—that pause people experience when sizing each other up for the first time—Boise was having quite a lengthy negotiation with God.

God stretched across the driveway in front of Cowboy. "Boise, my young son!" He beamed, throwing His hand out in front of Himself. "I haven't heard from you in a while. How have you been?"

"Just great, Lord," Boise responded, taking God's hand and shaking it vigorously.

"Whoa there, tough guy. You could hurt someone shaking their hand that way," He joked, pretending to wince. He reached down and took Boise's elbow with His left hand. "Listen," He said. "I need you to do something for Me."

"Sure, Boss. Anything you want," Boise answered without hesitation.

"I need you to kind of take this one under your wing for a while," He said.

"Mind if I ask why?" Now there was a moment of pause in his voice, and the longer he scrutinized this scrawny six-year-old, the more reason he had to pause.

"Well, I'm afraid I promised him someone to take his mind off the little things," God explained. "Actually, I promised him three *someones* last night. You happen to be the first on my list."

"Who else you got on that list?" Boise asked through a chuckle.

God looked in his eyes. "Do I need anyone else?"

"Well...no. Whatcha got in mind?"

"I just want you to show him some fun. You know what I mean; fishing, hunting, berry picking, arrowheads. I want you to do what you love to do, and just take him with you. Unlock the boy's soul and teach him that life is meant to be enjoyed. You know the drill."

"You mean you want me to make him my nephew," Boise said, pursing his lips and furrowing his brow a little, as if considering all of the facets of this little project. "You say you want me to take him under my wing for a *while*. Just how long is this *while*?"

"It's only for a single lifetime. Hardly a blink of an eye, really," God explained with a sly half smile.

"I don't know," Boise said, scrutinizing the boy a little closer. "Look at him. He looks like he just got out of bed no more than an hour ago and it's already a quarter to eight. His clothes are way too big; makes him look like he's got a tapeworm. His face is all dirty and his hair looks like it was licked by a horse. He's way too skinny and his legs are too long. His nose is runny and he..." Boise lifted his nose in the air and sniffed deeply, "he stinks like Vicks."

"Since when do you care what anyone looks like?" God rolled His eyes in a smile. "And the Vicks is because he has a touch of hay fever. His momma puts it on him."

"Hay fever! No way!" Boise wanted to sound convincing, but sure didn't want to be caught yelling at the boss. "You know the kind of life I lead, and it ain't got no room for anyone suffering from hay fever. Why I can just hear him snorting and sneezing in the middle of a spring turkey hunt now," Boise whined.

God smiled a little. "C'mon, Boise. I'll take care of the hay fever whenever he's with you." God knew He didn't have to negotiate, but He wanted Boise to enjoy this adventure as well. He also knew that Boise didn't like taking orders. He was hoping the Army would have helped with that, but for some reason, it only seemed to make matters worse. Boise disliked taking orders more than ever before, although he had shown that he could. God nodded at him patiently and thought to Himself, *That was the point, after all.*

"Awright," Boise agreed, "but it'll cost ya."

"What's your price?" God asked. This was a kind of ritual that He and Boise went through on occasion. He figured He might as well entertain him with it for a while.

"Well, for starters, I don't want to miss another hunting season, and this season, I want to bag the biggest whitetail buck in camp."

Boise tilted his head down a little wondering what he could get away with in this negotiation.

"Is that it?" God asked.

"Oh, no...no way. This looks to be a helluva project you're getting me into," Boise explained. "I'm headed out to Miracle Mile for a few weeks this summer and I want a full creel every day. And I don't mean those three-quarter pounders you threw at me last time I was there. I want some really nice fish."

"You got it," God agreed. "It'll be a perfect starting point for your new project when you bring that boy with you." God's grin was barely wide enough to contain the thunderous laughter trying to erupt.

Boise had a look of mild disgust on his face. He hadn't planned on having anyone tag along with him to Miracle Mile. "Oh, and one more thing," he added, knowing perfectly well that his luck had already been pushed.

"Boise," God admonished through His smile, "you want me to call your momma?" God laughed, knowing this would quiet him down. If Grandma came out there and saw that skinny kid standing there, she would pack him full of food and force him onto Boise. "Take them boys fishin', Boise!" she would yell. While Boise had an acute distain for taking orders, he knew better than to even flinch when his momma was issuing them.

"No, no, no, now." Boise was holding up both hands in front of his chest in a *let's calm down* fashion. "There's no need to get her involved in this. I'll settle for the big buck, no more missed seasons, and two weeks' worth of four-pound rainbows," Boise said with his nose pointed toward the ground and his eyes looking up, wondering if he got away with it.

"Boi-see." God laughed as if He'd just caught a child in the cookie jar.

"Awright. Three-pounders," Boise sighed, "but he better damn well be worth the trouble." He was feigning agitation. "Hay fever indeed" he added in a way some snob might note that they had just run out of hand towels at the country club.

"It's a deal then," God chimed with a great, toothy grin. "Congratulations on your new nephew, my boy!" God seemed very pleased when He took Boise's hand and shook it vigorously. "And since you tried to shake me down a little there, I've decided to call her out anyway."

"NO!" Boise protested. "There's no need to get her invol..." He never got to finish before God kissed him on the brow and walked away.

"Thanks, Boise. I knew I could count on you." As God walked away, He looked down at the dirty-faced little boy wearing clothes that were two sizes too big. He ran His fingers through the boy's hair and said over His shoulder, "And don't worry. This one is well worth it."

With the moment passed, Boise looked at Cowboy standing on the dirt drive in the morning sun. "This is my partner, Cowboy!" Gary was still yelling and whooping. "C'mere, Cowboy! This is my uncle Boise!"

Boise threw out his hand and closed the distance between them in a single step. Cowboy took his hand and shook it as vigorously as he knew how. Boise bent at the knees a little and pretended to wince. "Whoa there, tough guy!" he yelped. "You're gonna hurt somebody shaking their hand like that!" Boise reached down and took the boy's elbow in his left hand.

"Howdy, Uncle Boise," Cowboy said as politely as he knew. Gary's excitement was contagious and Cowboy was beginning to be convinced; he was shaking the hand of the most amazing man on earth.

"Uncle Boise indeed," Boise repeated, just as his mother threw the front screen door open.

"Who's out there with you, Boise?" she yelled.

"It's Gary the Fish Killer, and this..." he took Cowboy by the chin and looked deeply into his crisp hazel eyes, "...this wild man," he finished in a softly fading voice.

"Well, get 'em in here for crying out loud. They look half starved. I just cooked up some deer sausage and eggs and pancakes." She ran her fingers through Cowboy's hair in a way that felt strangely familiar to him, and added, "And I got some fresh chokecherry syrup that you can put on the cakes."

"Yum," Boise said with a smile. "Ya got any of that for me?"

"Well, of course I do, Boy." Boise's mother laughed as she tousled his hair. "When you're done eatin', you can take them boys fishing."

III. Open His Mind

Boise's rules were simple. Rule number one: enjoy yourself. Rule number two: if possible, enjoy yourself even more. Rule number three was rarely referenced, but when Boise saw that the first two rules were being ignored, he ensured rule number three was fully enforced, which typically found him, Gary, and Cowboy bleeding from several places and sore from their belly buttons to their cheekbones from all the laughing.

Boise fulfilled his assignment to the best of his ability and with the utmost joy. Over the years, when Cowboy was in his care, Boise taught him that people are often difficult, but life didn't have to be. If left to itself, life was beautiful, delicate, and even joyous.

Cowboy could never be certain that Boise would realize how much he was loved, but he came to know how much Boise loved him when he told the young man one day, "Wherever I have a dry place to sleep, a piece of it belongs to you." Their adventures were a respite for Cowboy where anything could, and often did happen, and through it all, Boise never laid a hand on him in anger.

It was nearly thirty years and a surreal childhood, from which Uncle Boise had rescued Cowboy on countless occasions, before *The Second* appeared. Cowboy had pulled a six-year stint in what Boise referred to as "The Navy Place," studying engineering and machinery. They often exchanged letters and continue to do so to this day.

Cowboy read every book he could get his hands on while enlisted, and had been sent to numerous engineering schools by keeping his Chief Engineering Officer convinced that he would re-enlist. He never did, and never regretted it. He never lived in Wyoming again and only visited occasionally, during which, Boise would nod at him in understanding and tell him, "It appears you have it all knowed up now."

Cowboy had met Dan when he took a job assessing machinery risks for an insurance company. They had developed a close professional relationship and Dan mentored him for several years. Although Cowboy had a great admiration for Dan, he did not feel that he was there to teach him any great, personal revelation. Dan had been hinting to Cowboy for some time about developing his skills in the larger, industrial settings, but it wasn't until Cowboy actually agreed to undertake the task that things got interesting for him.

Dan and Cowboy were driving toward the power plant where Cowboy was to begin initial training. Cowboy's youthful confidence convinced him that he pretty much had the whole power generation thing "all knowed up," and he didn't anticipate learning much more than he could by enduring five dollars' worth of overdue library fines, but he would go through the motions and keep everyone smiling. Cowboy's biggest problem was that, at that age, he knew so much more than he understood, and no amount of reading was ever going to prepare him for what he was about to learn.

Dan threw the car in park and the two of them strolled to the facility offices, where Dan informed him, "Duane can teach you anything if you can get him to talk. He's a brilliant person who has been doing this for nearly twenty years, so when he talks to you, listen carefully." Dan had a sly smile of his own when preparing Cowboy to meet Duane.

They entered the plant complex and Dan spied Duane in the manager's office, smiled at him, and headed that direction. Duane caught a glimpse of Dan, smiled, and stood to greet him, covering the entire distance across the manager's office in one stride. He took Dan's hand and pumped it like a man at a water well with a powerful thirst.

Duane was in his mid-forties, six-foot-seven, and every bit of a solidly assembled 270 pounds. He defined the word "looming." He was enormous.

"I've got someone here I want you to work with for a while," Dan told him. "He's a pretty bright kid, but he's a little rough."

"Rough! Good Lord," Duane jibed playfully, as if Cowboy wasn't even there, "he looks like a wild man."

"Duane, this is Cowboy. Cowboy, Duane," Dan introduced, grinning now at the expression on Cowboy's face. He looked as if someone had just informed him that he was pregnant.

Cowboy had never seen anyone so large move so gracefully. *Whew!* he thought. *I never knew these animals could get this big.*

"Cowboy?!" Duane said with subdued bewilderment. "How did you come across a name like that?"

"I picked it up as a kid and it just kind of stuck," Cowboy admitted.

"Well, what should I call you?"

"Oh, I don't know," Cowboy paused for effect. "How about *Cowboy?*" he finished with a mild smart-assed grin.

Duane closed the distance between them, shoving his hand out to take Cowboy's. It was that brilliant pause two people have when sizing each other up for the first time. Cowboy could almost read Duane's furrowing mind as he reached for his hand: *Oh, Lord, this kid is not ready.*

"But I think he is," God announced and He stepped between their extended hands.

"Oh, I don't know, Lord." Duane didn't call God by any pet names like "Boss." He seemed to have a much higher regard for The Creator. "He's so-oo young, and he's got a look about him that makes me a little nervous."

"What kind of a look?"

"Kind of a crazy look...like a wild man."

"I know. It's one of the things I find most endearing about him. He is, in many respects, untamable, and I'd like to keep it that way."

"Well, then why have You brought him here to me, Lord?"

"I need your help with a little project I started many years ago when I promised this young man that I would send three. For him

---

to completely know that I am at work here, I must send him the three," God explained.

"And which am I, Lord?" Duane asked, without taking his eyes off Cowboy.

"You, sir, are number two," God grinned, "but vital to this project." Apparently, God held Duane in pretty high regard as well.

"And what is it you would like me to do with him?" Duane asked, becoming even more curious.

"Open his mind," God told him matter-of-factly.

"OH! NO!" Duane sounded terribly upset. "You can't possibly think that I am capable of teaching this smart aleck how to consider...how to learn...to understand. I'm certain that you've got the wrong man for the job."

"Well, you are at the top of my list, and if I remember correctly, you did make promises regarding your sobriety, your three sons, that whole wisdom thing you were asking for." God smiled at Duane even brighter.

"Who else might you have on that list, Lord? I'm sure they will have a much better chance at this kid than I ever will." Duane sounded like a teenager who was just asked to shovel snow off the driveway.

"Everyone else on the list is otherwise occupied at the moment." God pretended to read off names on a small notepad He was holding. "Let's see, there's Nietzsche; he's with Me, and Plato; also with Me, and Dionne Junior, who still has a little penance to pay for that whole Clinton fiasco... Nope. Sorry, sir. It looks like you're it. Besides," He added smiling wider, "you are at the top of My list, and I only want the best for this kid."

Even as teenagers shoveling snow out of driveways know to do, Duane succumbed. "As you wish, Lord."

"Try not to look at it as a chore, sir. I am entrusting one of My children into the hands of one of My favorite people. Besides," He added, "there is a reward in it for you."

"I have all the reward I could ever hope for in Your presence, Lord." Duane's chest inflated just slightly and his shoulders went back. "But...well...since you brought it up." He looked like a middle school boy trying to ask a cheerleader to the dance.

God's shoulders swayed with His contained laughter. "He will make you laugh. He will make you think. He will call you 'Father.' And wherever he has a dry place to sleep, you will own a piece of it."

"It doesn't sound like much," Duane pouted. Then, muttering so softly he couldn't even hear himself, he added, "He'd better be worth it."

God bent down, kissed Duane on the brow, and turned to leave. On His way out, He stopped beside the young man and ran His fingers through the thick brown mane on his head and added, "Thank you, Duane, and don't worry. He's worth it."

Cowboy felt the bones grinding in his hand as Duane squeezed, throwing it up and down like a Handyman jack. *If he ever had a flat,* Cowboy thought looking straight up at Duane's firmly set jawline, *I'm betting the jack is optional.*

"Good to meet you," Duane said. But he didn't sound like it was very good at all. Cowboy thought he might as well have been saying, "Go to hell, you little bastard," or "You ate the last piece of cheesecake, you creep."

Something happened to Cowboy just then that hadn't happened in many years. He was intimidated. Duane had a voice that could be felt. He was serious, to the point, and left no doubt as to where a person stood with him. He found Cowboy mildly irritating, and Cowboy knew it.

Boise taught Cowboy a lot of things over the years; important things, like the best time to shoot a whitetail buck is right when you see him. The best way to keep the house clean is to never let it get dirty. The best way to keep your knife sharp is to never let it get dull. And the best time to poke a sleeping grizzly is *never.* Cowboy had an ominous feeling that this bear had just been poked.

"Give him what he needs," Dan told Duane. "Like I said, he's got a good mind, but he could stand a little polish." Dan grinned widely as he left the manager's office, still amused at the expression left on Cowboy's face. Dan spent the rest of the day with them, but returned to Minneapolis later that afternoon. Cowboy kept to himself while wandering the plant with them that day, leaving all the talking to Dan and Duane. They were old friends and enjoyed each other, and aside from the occasional discerning eye that Cowboy received from Duane, the rest of the day was uneventful.

They went to dinner that evening under the casual discussion of work. Duane rarely divulged any information not requested, and very limited information when it was. He seemed to be studying Cowboy, getting a feel for his disposition, his attitude. They talked about their military backgrounds, how they came to work for the company, and other menial, unimportant topics. At the end of the day, Cowboy knew as much about Duane as when the day had started. He had a strange feeling, however, that Duane knew everything there was to know about him since the day he was born.

The following day was filled with as much tedium as the first. Cowboy would ask Duane questions of a technical nature, and Duane would answer in as few words as possible. Dinner that evening found them discussing other things that were related to work only in topic. The essence of their conversation ran much deeper.

"How do you like this kind of work," Duane asked through his boredom.

"I enjoy the work a lot," Cowboy answered. Then he hesitated, trying to decide if he should complete his thoughts on how he genuinely felt. "It always strikes me as odd how a majority of the problems we are faced with seem to originate within the company."

Surprise splashed across Duane's face and he perked up immediately. "What do you mean?"

"It just seems to me," Cowboy started sheepishly, "that all of the problems we hear about regarding reporting, level of service, quality of service, value of service, and so on, are only problems to us. I have not heard a client issuing a complaint yet."

Duane smiled. "What has brought you to such enlightened conclusions?"

"Casual observation" was all Cowboy replied. He was beginning to enjoy talking to Duane because Duane spoke to him like an adult and used words like "enlightened." It somehow reminded Cowboy of his father.

"Why do you suppose it is that this company complains so openly about the manner in which we perform our duties?" Duane insisted.

"Because they would rather we didn't work for them," Cowboy replied. "At the very least, they wish they could get someone else to pay for our input. I don't expect it is that uncommon, really, but it is disheartening."

"Now why is that?" Duane asked, again showing real interest.

"I suspect it is because we are engineers. We are simply there to sway the odds of insuring a large industrial exposure into their favor. If they could somehow manage to acquire the same gambling odds without enduring the engineering expense associated with it, they would have considerably more money to gamble with, instead of using it to pay our salaries." Cowboy was to the point, and Duane was beginning to enjoy talking with him as well.

"Do you believe in God?"

Duane's question stunned Cowboy. It seemed like a theological sneak attack in the midst of casual conversation, and although Cowboy slightly stiffened with nerves, he did not hesitate with his answer.

"Yes. I cannot be certain who you mean by God, but I believe there must be more than this." Cowboy turned his head, nodding at the restaurant.

The next question Duane posed made him very excited, so much so that he wanted to get closer to Cowboy and look into his eyes when he asked. He leaned forward a little, peered at Cowboy through a thick intensity, and asked, "Why?"

"Because the evidence I have seen does not support the statement that we belong here," Cowboy answered flatly.

"What evidence might that be?"

"Bipedal motivation is a completely unnatural means of self-transportation. It is injurious to a person's feet, knees, spine, neck...

it doesn't make sense that, under the rules of nature, we should just evolve into such an unnatural condition. We are not subject to the rules of nature, and often break those rules to its detriment and our gain. Sure, there are times that nature takes a shot back, but by and large, we rule nature, not the other way around."

"Perhaps we evolved to such a higher level of intellectual capacity that we command nature," Duane retorted.

"Perhaps, but that does not explain our origination, only our growth. Nature cannot create beyond itself. It cannot create something by applying its rules, and have that something turn around only to break those very rules. Everything I have studied in nature lives under the rules of which it was created, regardless of its own evolutionary path, with only one exception...us."

"Fascinating," Duane whispered. "So you are convinced that, because we do not belong here..."

"Right. We must belong somewhere else. At least that would paraphrase my more scientific answer." Cowboy extended.

"What other answer might you have?" Duane was smiling broadly at this point.

"A more philosophical one. Impossible to substantiate, but thought-provoking, nonetheless."

"Let's hear it," Duane insisted. "What are you waiting for?"

"I normally try desperately not to be too provoking," Cowboy admitted, "particularly with someone as large as you."

Duane finally laughed out loud. He had a booming, free laugh that Cowboy found frightening and infectious, so Cowboy joined him nervously. "I promise I won't sit on you for anything as evasive as philosophy," Duane vowed through his subsiding laugh.

"Well," Cowboy started as his own laughter ebbed, "after reading a lot of different views on the subject, I concluded that whether God created us or we created Him, we must concede that either we both exist, or neither of us do, since that is the very essence of creation."

Duane gave Cowboy's perspective an intense moment of thought and then smugly remarked, "Perhaps I believe in fairies.

Since I believe in them, I have created them, and therefore they must exist."

"Maybe you'd have a better chance of getting me to believe that if you were covered in dust, wearing wings, and spouting a theory that the great fairy is the creator of the universe. If any of those things were true, then I would be compelled to listen. We are an unnatural creature on this earth. To paraphrase, you might say that God created us in His own image, which is why we do not belong here. Or that we created God to suit our image, which is still unnatural to this earth. In either case, we have either created or been created outside of the limitation of this earth, or we are just figments of each other's imaginations."

Duane sat back in his chair, rubbing his chin. "Interesting," he muttered.

Their conversation at the restaurant in nowhere Minnesota that evening solidified the deepest of friendships and opened a line of discourse that they knew would last them the rest of their lives. At conferences, meetings, training seminars, and any chance or planned encounter, the two would spend hours discussing God, men, heaven, hell, earth, Christ, children, parenting, society, government, business, culture, and all things in between.

Duane invoked the deepest thoughts from Cowboy and taught him how to consider everything. "Don't just buy a book and read it," Duane would instruct. "Before you buy a book, think about how it is marketed, study the author and learn why he wrote it, consider the verbiage the author chose as he wrote the book, think about the impact the book might have to you or anyone else who might read it and whatever their circumstances might be. Consider the book deeply before you buy it."

"It seems such a simple thing," Duane warned, "but it is coming to be a rarity in the world today. People will do and say and see things surrounding them daily and not give them a second thought." Once he finished teaching Cowboy how to consider his thoughts, his actions, and his surroundings, he taught him how to relate those considerations to the rest of the world.

"Relate your considerations to everyone and everything else around and within you. How are those relationships important or unimportant to you personally? How might they relate to mankind? How would the lack of those relationships impact you?" Duane was relentless. Cowboy was delighted. Duane had encouraged this moderately intelligent young man how to wonder, insisted that he fascinate, and taught him to perceive. It was brilliant and miraculous for them both.

They spent the next three weeks together under the guise of risk assessment training and within a few days of returning to their homes, Duane called a delighted Cowboy.

"What are you doing?" Duane asked.

"Wondering," Cowboy responded.

"And have you discovered any answers?"

"Who can know," Cowboy answered amidst the laughter. "But I have discovered that having the answers is not nearly as fun as finding them."

"You are a remarkable young man."

"And you, sir, are a remarkable teacher. Thank you, Father," Cowboy responded and hung up the phone to anxiously await their next conversation.

IV. To Open His Heart

Cowboy remembered that little girl so many years before, pinching his ear and rhyming. With Duane hovering so near and Boise so ingrained within, he spent the next decade just looking and listening. He knew, deep in his bones, that the words spoken by his sleepy twin were not just the utterings of a sleep-talking child who had seen too many episodes of old sitcoms. It was something that riddled him with questions, ideas, searches, and investigations throughout his life.

He plodded on, living typically, and began to consider that perhaps he'd been mistaken. *There was no* three, he caught himself thinking more and more often. *Or maybe there was a three, but he missed him. Walked right by him and never took notice*, he would think. *Got caught with my pants down, juggling the tasks of life, and now he's gone, never to offer the third gift.*

Contrary to Duane's delight, Cowboy found himself sulking in a college classroom again. He sat passively chatting with other students about things of no importance. He found it pleasantly social, until he heard a voice from behind him. It was not a laughing, robust voice. It was not verbose or thundering. In fact, it was extraordinarily soothing. It was the voice of a woman.

It came from the doorway at his back that led into the classroom. Upon hearing it, Cowboy felt a tickling over the back of his neck, like a mouse with cold feet had just run up his spine. The thick brown hair on the back of his head stood on end, and he noticeably straightened and inhaled sharply through his teeth.

"Oh, I know! I just love that!"

Cowboy turned around toward the door, but with the flood of students entering, he couldn't be sure which of them spoke in such a way. Shortly, everyone was seated and the instructor passed around a blank sheet of paper. Everyone was to pen their names, phone numbers, and email addresses on the page as it passed by.

As it was handed to Cowboy, he looked carefully at the names that had been listed on it to that point. He wasn't sure what to think. Maybe the name of whoever owned that voice would blink in purple or something. He knew it was owned by a woman, but all of them looked so young. He found the voices of young women to be many things, but would never have described any of them as soothing.

Once the list was completed, the instructor made copies for everyone and then asked for the traditional timid verbal introductions that each student must endure. As each in attendance began their brief biographies, Cowboy heard little of interest and began to excuse the cause of the spine-tingling phenomenon as a draft stirred by the swinging door or coming from a leaking window. He was beginning to guess that the previous years of looking had made him a little anxious to meet this third gift.

Then to his left he heard, "Hello. I'm Kyle. I work at the state facility in the southern part of the state." Cowboy snapped his head in the direction of this voice. There it was.

He heard it again. It was not the words she spoke. They were typical, uneventful words perfunctory in these settings. It was not in the delivery of the words; also pretty routine. But the voice... what he heard in her voice was enthusiasm, kindness, security, truth, honesty, clarity...he heard what he suspected to be joy.

As much as what he heard in that voice was what he did not hear. He did not hear disdain, superficiality, discouragement, confusion, or insincerity. He had engaged in thousands of conversations with people all over the world and would have liked to think that he, at least, had a measurable discernment of detecting and defining voice fluctuations that were meaningful to some extent, regardless of how little. And he was enthralled by this voice saying nothing to complete strangers.

Now, that really didn't mean much to Cowboy, as he had been enthralled lots of times. He assured himself that she was undoubtedly very interesting. She couldn't have been more than a hundred pounds and, he guessed, only came to about his shoulder. Probably in her early to mid-thirties and absolutely lovely, he thought, sitting across the classroom wondering if he was staring.

He put her out of his mind for the remainder of the class but decided that he would talk to her afterward just to say hello or something socially mechanical. Once the class ended, he watched her don her coat and gloves. He strolled across the room to briefly introduce himself. As he did so, he looked into her eyes.

They reminded him of a swimming pond he frequented as a boy on hot summer days. The heat and humidity would drive him, Boise, and Gary to strip and dive into the clear, cool satisfaction of instant relief. He wanted to dive into her eyes.

Being so much taller, he looked down at her petite frame and thought, *She's incredibly strong for someone so small.*

She looked up and smiled in a way that he could only describe as radiating. He heard himself inhale sharply again. The trite verbiage of so many long dead poets could not do it justice, but he found her stunningly beautiful and deliciously infatuating.

"Well, hello," she said in that wonderful voice. She reached out her gloved hand to take his as they were sizing each other up, and in that ever-miraculous moment—that pause people experience from just knowing when meeting each other—God stepped in.

He didn't take her hand. He practically draped His arm around her like a shawl. He pulled her in and kissed her on her brow and said, "Hello, Kyle."

"Oh, Lord! It's Him! It's You! He's here!" She sounded like a teenager at a Beatles concert. For a moment, God thought she would start jumping straight up and down from all the excitement. He loved it when she did that.

"How are you doing, My love?" God asked.

"I'm just wonderful," she exclaimed in a way that left no doubt that she was genuinely wonderful. "What brings you here?" she asked, again in a way that left no reason to think she wanted to know anything but why God was there.

"Well," He said, "I was wondering if you would consider doing me a favor?" As He asked, He slipped around behind her, leaving her to face a rather tall stranger who appeared to be...well...sparkling.

"Of course!" she agreed before He even finished his sentence. "Of course, I'll do it!" she repeated with such enthusiasm.

"You are simply one of my most favorite," He announced. "I knew you would. In fact, you were the only one on my list." He slipped His arm around her waist, bent low, and put His lips right behind her right ear. His cheek was cool against the side of her neck. He pulled her in tightly. She loved it when God did this. It made her feel safe.

God raised His hand in front of her, on her right, and pointed directly at this tall stranger. He whispered into the back of her ear, "Take a look at him." Kyle, through her cool swimming pond eyes and beaming smile, tucked into the security of God's arm, looked at the man. The only thing she could think was that he looked like a wild man.

"I want you to open his heart."

"Open his heart?!" Kyle was a bit flabbergasted.

"Yes. This man has undergone a lifetime of difficulties and never known unconditional love. He is convinced that it does not exist. He has ignored his hopes and dreams and has done everything the world has told him that was good and right and just, but he still does not understand. His soul does not belong to the world. It belongs to Me," God whispered.

She stood, warmly pondering the man. "How on earth am I supposed to open his heart? I wouldn't even know where to begin to do something like that!"

"Then do not start with anything of this earth." God moved around and stood facing her. He brushed the hair above her left ear back, running His fingers through it. "I know you're not a name dropper, but if you tell him you know Me, you'll be amazed at how easy this will be."

Oh, Lord! she thought. *If I put together everything I've ever known and everything I've ever done, I'll never come up with a way to casually mention God to this wild man.*

"You'll be surprised. I promise," God said, looking directly through her eyes. She was moderately shocked by the way He answered her thoughts.

Be careful, she thought.

"No," He insisted. "Don't be careful. The last thing I want you to do is be careful. Instead, be mindful and open. And, just in case you're wondering," God continued as He slid His hand up the back of her neck and pulled her closer. He bent and pressed His cheek to her and whispered so deeply that she felt it, "he's worth it."

Then she got the joke. "Just in case I was wondering," she said as clearly as she could while belly-laughing. "Just ...hahahaha...in case I was...AAHAAAA...HAHAHA...wondering...HAHAHAHAHAHA!" She couldn't believe that God had a sense of humor. "He knows everything and just finished reading my thoughts, and then He says, 'just in case you were wondering.'" and as she finished the thought, she started laughing again.

God stood there giggling, waiting for her laughter to subside. When she finally regained control of her hysterics, she reached up and patted Him on the chest. "You are too funny!" she told Him through a brilliant smile.

"Well, you will wonder," he told her, still grinning Himself, "but not today. Actually, not for some time yet, but the day will come when you will wonder." He bent down again and kissed Kyle directly between the eyebrows. He held her there for a brief moment, feeling the warmth of her forehead against His lips and hugging her deeply. "Thank you so much for doing this for me, Kyle. You are truly one of my most favorites."

"You always make it abundantly clear that the pleasure is all mine," she told Him, causing Him to laugh out loud. His laugh was booming and free. There wasn't the slightest reservation to it.

He turned to leave, and as He stepped up to the man's side, He paused. God leaned slightly toward the man's right ear and said, "As I have promised, here is the third. This one will remind you that I have made the entire universe just for you. Everything that ever was, everything there is, and all that is yet to come belongs to you. Let me see what you do with it." And He brushed His fingers through the man's thick brown hair that was lightened with sparse graying.

Cowboy felt the gloved hand of this young woman daintily fall into his. He wasn't sure he would be able to withstand the brilliance of her smile to look into her eyes. She was blinding. When her hand met his, he managed a glimpse into her eyes and he distinctly remembered wishing that she wasn't wearing gloves. He wanted to feel her skin as he swam into her beautifully clear eyes.

The cold-footed mouse that ran up his spine earlier had called all of his friends and they were happily dancing all over him when her eyes met his. He was convinced that he was holding the hand of the most amazing creature on the earth.

He stood there betting himself that this woman probably knew God personally. *Of course*, he thought. *She probably has Him as speed-dial one on her cell phone.*

2

A STILL, SMALL VOICE

I.

The Good Reverend Bodean hung up the phone and scurried quickly down the hall. In reaching its end, he peeked around the door frame of the church secretary's office and whispered, scratching his short gray beard against the oak sill as he did.

Annabelle didn't raise her head at all. She was busy studying the church budget when she peered over the horn-rimmed glasses that barely hung on the end of her nose. "What?" she barked. She could tell Jimmy was excited. Annabelle remembered meeting Jimmy Bodean on the second day of kindergarten. He did not attend the first day, as he was recovering from a bout with mumps. Annabelle knew this because he announced it to the seven five-year-olds in the class and Mrs. Gulley, the kindergarten through third grade teacher.

Little Jimmy Bodean had a tremendous crush on Mrs. Gulley, and Annabelle noticed that whenever Mrs. Gulley spoke to Jimmy, he clasped his hands tightly together, holding them against his chest, and he whispered. Although she had seen this behavior several more times, Annabelle hadn't related the level of Jimmy's excitement to the softness of his voice until seventh grade, when he asked his future bride, Rose, to the street dance. The more excited

Jimmy was, the softer he spoke. To ask her for the date, he simply carried a flyer announcing the street dance clutched tightly to his chest as he marched up to Rose. She looked at the flyer just below Jimmy's radiant smile, laid her hand on the back of his, and said, "Of course I'll go to the dance with you."

Annabelle always thought it very odd that he became the Lutheran minister for this sleepy little Nebraska town, but his unusual whispering was never a problem while speaking in public, even in kindergarten. The truth was that the good reverend hadn't had much to be excited about since Rose's passing nearly eight years ago. The whispering faded with his wife and his excitement, except for a brief period of it last year.

And here it was again today. "What did you say?" Annabelle asked even louder.

Reverend Bodean stood in front of Annabelle's office door. His wide, toothy grin showed through the white October beard he grew every year for the church Christmas pageant. The grizzled itch of the stubble found his fingers softly clawing at his chest now. "Cowboy's coming," he whispered louder, followed by a squeaking "Tee-hee."

"Cowboy? Who the hell... Oh, Lord." Annabelle's expression changed from pinched curiosity to a mild slacking shock, forcing her glasses to slip off the end of her nose. She took no notice of the thin gold chain jerking her horn-rimmed glasses to a stop directly above her enormous breasts. "Is that the fella who did the boiler last year?" The tone of her voice began a slight crescendo as she asked, exposing her concern. She regained herself and calmly advised, "You might want to steer clear of this Cowboy character this time around, Jimmy. I'll take care of this."

"Nonsense." The reverend was still excited, but clearly under control and audible. He straightened his spine in the office doorway. "In our current financial situation, I need to help in every way possible around here," Jimmy explained through a mischievous grin.

Annabelle leaned forward in her chair, interlocking her fingers and setting her elbows on the heavy oak desk that the elementary school donated to the church fifteen years before. She peered seriously into the bright blue eyes of Reverend Bodean. "You know the last time he was here, it took you nearly a month to recover your normal tone of voice. Don't think the church admin board didn't take notice, Mr. Jimmy Bodean." Annabelle always called him that to offer a gauge of how serious she was. She had done it their entire lives, and now she wanted to remind him that the church's administrative board had the authority to terminate him, should he be unable to perform his duties. Whispering through a month of sermons would certainly qualify.

The reverend bent slowly over, placing his hands on his knees. Deep laughter was squeaking out of him, carried by a full breath of air. His shoulders and head began to bob rhythmically as the squeaking oscillated on the ebbing flow of his breath. He stood, sucking another breath of air from above his head, and, nothing like the smoker's laugh that just left him, he guffawed loudly, holding his belly. "Annie," he gasped at another breath, "you *are* the admin board."

After hearing himself actually say it, he laughed even harder. "He'll be here Wednesday," Reverend Bodean informed her as he turned and laughed his way back to his own office. He was nearly reaching an Eddie Murphy level of hysterics, wiping the back of his arm across his forehead, cradling his waist, with a lot of "AHH-HAHAHAHAH-ing" and "WOO-HOO-ing." As his laughter faded down the distance of the hallway, Annabelle heard him softly saying, "OH...that's funny. Woo."

Now standing with her hands on the teacher's desk, Annabelle yelled down the hall after him. "I'm the secretary and the treasurer too, Mr. Jimmy Bodean! That means you might want to start listening to me!" she bossed.

Accomplishing nothing more than throwing Reverend Bodean into another, even heartier bout of laughter, Annabelle snatched her horn-rims off her breasts and poked them back on her nose. As she plopped back down on her seat, her eyes were scanning her desk for nothing in particular. She began rearranging the papers strewn about and through her tightly pursed lips she muttered, "I don't care for that...that...*wild man!*" she said with as much disdain as she could muster over the faint, distant hilarity emanating from Jimmy's office. "I don't care for him one bit."

II.

Cowboy hung up the phone and leaned far back in his heavy padded desk chair, scratching his head vigorously with both hands. He had been subcontracting himself out to the state to help them catch up on the backlog of overdue inspections over the last few years. He found the work tedious, but it provided a decent supplemental income.

The chief inspector of the state tried to hire him several times, but after six years of active military service, Cowboy couldn't be less interested in government work at any level. Since Cowboy liked the Chief, he was willing to help out as a consultant where he could until they got caught up. Since the Chief trusted Cowboy, he pulled some strings, called in his favors, and made the special arrangements needed to allow him to bring on an independent consultant. It wasn't perfect, but it was a win-win Band-Aid.

Cowboy had misplaced the memory of Reverend Bodean for nearly a year, but found it the instant he proposed a schedule for the boiler inspection to him on the phone. He thought they had become disconnected when he told the reverend that he'd like to come out on Wednesday to look at the boiler. Once he held the cordless to his ear a little tighter, Cowboy could hear the good reverend softly whispering on the other end.

Oh yeah, Cowboy thought, *the whispering minister*. He hoped he hadn't offended the reverend with his soft chuckle, but Cowboy couldn't help himself. He didn't have a handle on the nature of Reverend Bodean's whispering phenomenon, and Cowboy didn't figure it was relevant, but it was a bit comical. "I can't hear you very well, Reverend. We must have a bad connection," Cowboy announced.

"Wednesday's fine," was all he said, and it took every effort on Cowboy's part to hear it.

"I'll see you first thing Wednesday morning then, Reverend." Offering his thanks, Cowboy hung up the phone, scratched his head again, and crossed his Double H riding boots on the corner of his desk. *The whispering minister*, he thought again. *What'll they invent next?*

Cowboy rummaged through the filing cabinets and rifled through the stacks cluttering his mind and finally landed on the memory details of last year's meeting with Jimmy Bodean. He laced his fingers behind his head and remembered instantly liking this man. *He had a brilliant smile.* Cowboy's thoughts pooled around the image of Reverend Bodean standing on the front steps of the church. *Yes. Yes. White hair and a white beard that only made his smile look whiter...kind of a small stature...and saddened eyes that seemed to betray their happy, sparkling blue color.*

Cowboy's chair complained with a creak as he leaned it back to the razor's edge of balance. He closed his eyes and his shoulders relaxed after the successful search for the memory of last year's visit with Reverend Bodean. *Ah, yes,* his recollection whispered from the back of his mind. *we had a great conversation that had nothing at all to do with boilers.*

III.

The white Ford Ranger slipped unnoticed through the sleepy little town in central Nebraska. Cowboy flipped the turn signal up indicating to the empty street his intention of making a right on Jefferson Avenue, the main drag of this tidy little village of about eight thousand souls. He tilted the brim of his Stetson just enough to shade his eyes from the sunrise spilling over the street.

He was early. The farmers had been working for an hour by then and everyone else had another hour and three more snooze buttons before scrambling out of bed. It was an unusually warm October morning. Dew glistened from the walnut and maple trees lining Jefferson Avenue as the sun continued its chore of re-coloring the leaves and encouraging them to let go. The dewy sparkling of reds, greens, and golds reminded Cowboy of a fireworks display as he rolled down the window to catch a deep autumn breath. He loved the smell of a Midwestern fall.

As he idled past the vacant City Hall in the center of the town square, he glanced at his clipboard to verify the contact name and address. It listed "Rev. J. A Bodean" as the contact name, and "Ah... there it is," he thought so suddenly that the words fell out of his mouth instead of remaining quietly trapped in his head. "Lincoln Street." This time the thought ricocheted quietly off the back of his closed teeth. *Keep your thoughts inside your head when you're alone, dummy.* The corner of his mouth curled slightly into a sly half smile as he said aloud, "I've got no patience for a man who drives around talking to himself." He chuckled through the left turn onto Lincoln Street thinking that at least he thought he was funny.

As he pulled in, he was a bit surprised to find two vehicles parked nose to nose in the paved lot in front of the church. "Maybe I'm not as early as I thought." He parked two slots away from the mid '70s Lincoln Continental while rolling up his window. He threw it in park just as the front left wheel hit the bottom of the pothole that found him. Snatching up his clipboard and sliding out of his seat, Cowboy paused to assess the pothole under the tire. *Jeez*, he thought. *Good thing I didn't fall in there. I'd need a damn grappling hook to climb back out.*

He ambled around the bed of his pickup and looked at the Lincoln. Mud was splashed up to the center line of the quarter panels. There were tissues scattered in the front seat and a front tractor tire standing up on the rear floorboard. Hanging from the rearview mirror was a photograph of a rather large woman holding the bill of a man's John Deere cap up to gain access to his face for a kiss. He was holding a bouquet of daisies, wearing a plaid flannel shirt and suspenders. The caption on the frame read "Happy 30th, Love Carl."

Cowboy continued his amble between his truck and the Lincoln. He paused for a moment to look at the full-sized Chevy van parked in front of the car. *Now this is interesting*, he thought. It was a boxy two-toned blue with a luggage rack loosely mounted to the top. The fender wells were rusted out, the paint was badly chipped, and the tires were frighteningly bald. Aside from a crack running from the bottom center across the passenger side of the windshield, the rest of the vehicle was immaculate.

Where there was paint, it was waxed and polished and glistening in the morning sun. Even the chrome ladder running up the back door to the luggage rack gleamed. Despite the crack, the windshield didn't even have a remnant of bug splatter. All the windows were spotless. The bald tires even had a nice Armor All shine to them.

Cowboy continued his stroll up the dozen concrete steps leading to the two front doors of the church that were left ajar; he entered the vestibule through the left door and glanced around while lifting off his hat. To the left were stairs leading to the basement. The vestibule was lined with a half a dozen finger paintings of nativity scenes, and a picture of the traditional blond-haired, blue-eyed Jesus on either side of the entryway.

He stepped through the swinging vestibule doors leading to the sanctuary and found stained glass windows down both sides, four aisles of heavy unpadded oak pews, with the standard issue wooden cross mounted on the wall behind the podium up on the altar. To the right of the altar was a fire exit and to the left was the passageway leading to the church offices. Cowboy's boots clunked heavily on the wooden floor of the center aisle as he headed for the offices.

Peering through the window of the first door on the right, Cowboy verified occupancy of the office upon seeing a very busty, middle-aged woman perched behind a heavy oak desk. She glanced over the top of horn-rimmed glasses when she saw movement in the window of her office door and, without lifting her head, raised her left hand and signaled Cowboy to come in by quickly squeezing her four extended fingers closed two times.

Cowboy swung the slightly opened door to the right and covered the distance to the front of Annabelle's desk in two long strides. "Howdy," he said while glancing around the room and shifting the hat and clipboard hanging from his left arm. He was admiring Annabelle's desk. It reminded him of the desk Miss Tavegee, his second-grade teacher, used. He had a terrible crush on Miss Tavegee that lasted until the third week of school, when she spanked him with a long, hardwood paddle for breaking every one of his crayons in half. Cowboy fixed his jaw firmly into a fierce gaze without making a sound through the spanking. How could she know that the boy only did it so he could share his crayons with his twin sister?

"Yes?" was Annabelle's response.

Seeing that this lady was all about the business at hand in spite of Cowboy's best effort at smiling, he continued, "I'm here to do the certificate inspection for your boiler."

Annabelle jerked the top right drawer of her desk open. Neatly hanging on tiny brass hooks screwed to the inside panel of the drawer were a dozen keys. She deftly plucked one from its hook and handed it to Cowboy without looking at him. "The boiler room is in the basement against the back wall. This key unlocks the gray door to get in. The certificate is hanging on the front of the boiler. If you have any problems you can talk with Reverend Bodean. His office is three doors down."

Whew, Cowboy thought. *This woman is wound tight*. Her office was modestly furnished and there wasn't one piece of paper out of place on any of the bookshelves, the top of the desk, or the desk drawer left open.

Annabelle caught him glancing in the desk drawer and shoved it closed. Looking at her computer screen over her glasses, she asked flatly, "Is there anything else?" She didn't care for these government types; invading the church, requiring inspections, and costing them money for repairs and certificates. She didn't like these types at all.

"No, ma'am," Cowboy answered, with another attempt at his best friendly smile, knowing how futile it would be. "Thank you." He marched back though the sanctuary down the aisle between the pews and the wall this time, admiring the stained glass windows along that wall of the church as he went.

His riding boots plodded loudly down the narrow staircase and carried him through the open basement littered with children's art paraphernalia. Using the key that Annabelle loaned him, he opened the gray metal door to the utility room. Finding it as dark as a coal mine, Cowboy pulled the Maglite from its holder on the right side of his belt and poked its button.

He scanned the room for a light switch when his beam finally lit upon a silver chain of beads hanging from a bare bulb in the center of the room. He gave it a light jerk, illuminating the utility room, and began the task at hand. He found the hot water storage tank, current certificate, and boiler resting neatly near the back of the room.

He completed all of his duties and verified conditions and documentation quickly. He thought again of how tedious these things had become, but did make a few notes to remind him to discuss the leaking flange on the main water piping and that it might be a good time to start planning to chemically clean the boiler.

He plucked at the light chain and locked the door on his way out. Reviewing his notes and filling out the paperwork found him back in Annabelle's office returning her key. "Everything seems to be in order and I'll submit a request to the state requesting that they issue a new certificate, but there were..." Cowboy's voice trailed off when Annabelle, without looking up from the Compaq 386, pointed her left index finger in the direction that would lead him down the hall.

"Three doors down," she said, as Cowboy gingerly placed the key on the front edge of her teacher's desk.

"Thank you, ma'am. It's been a real pleasure." The corners of Cowboy's mouth turned up into the grin of a boy who was up to no good as he was deciding whether or not he should continue. *Well, I just about have to do it, don't I?* he thought as his grin widened just enough to expose his front teeth.

He took a half side step to the left and bent at the waist slightly to enter Annabelle's field of peripheral vision. "And try not to worry too much about Carl. Harvest has always been a very stressful time for him, but you two have been through this many times over the last thirty years. You'll get that front tractor tire fixed for him while you're in town today, and he'll get the trunk latch fixed for you soon after harvest." Cowboy leaned a little farther in and stuffed his nose into the vase full of daisies beside Annabelle's computer screen. She finally turned her face toward this man in her office, and it had a look on it as if she had just sat on a whoopee cushion. "Daisies are my favorite flower too," he said after filling his nose with sweetness. "You know just how bad allergies can get, and this is one of the few flowers I'm not allergic to. Thanks again, ma'am."

Cowboy entered the narrow hallway with a giggle welling just under his breath. He didn't need to look to know that Annabelle was still staring toward him, frozen behind her desk with that same whoopee cushion expression locked on her face. He took a sharp right turn and strolled past the door for the ladies' room, then the men's room, and stopped to admire the little brass nameplate attached to the dark maple wood door tightly shut in front of him. "Rev. J. A. Bodean" was engraved in black against the dulled brass plate.

IV.

Cowboy gave the door a light rap. "Yes" he heard on the other side. He gave the antique glass knob a sharp underhanded turn with his right hand and entered Reverend Bodean's office. The room was dark except for the desk lamp. The air was dull and felt as sullen as a teenage boy. Reverend Bodean sagged in his large padded office chair, his forearms on the armrests, and his hands curled loosely around the ends of each of them. He seemed to be mesmerized by the Bible opened under the desk lamp in front of him. Reverend Bodean naturally assumed it was Annabelle coming to complain or boss him around, so he didn't raise his eyes from reading.

"Good morning, sir," Cowboy offered.

Jimmy jumped a little at the sound of an unfamiliar voice in his office, and turned in search of its source. "Well, good morning there," he said upon finding the tall figure in his doorway. As he rose from his chair and turned to greet Cowboy, he poked his hand out to the advancing figure and asked, "What can I do for you this morning?"

"I just wanted to review a few notes I made on the boiler inspection, and the secretary directed me to you." Cowboy took the reverend's hand and seemed to explore it. From the back of his mind he heard a thoughtful voice whisper, "Carefully now. This one is in pain." Cowboy peered deeply in the reverend's Caribbean blue eyes and lingered in his handshake for just a moment. The reverend's radiant smile faded slightly as he pondered the way men do when sizing each other up.

Cowboy noticed the slight fade of Jimmy's smile, the deep, vertical crease of worry between his thick white eyebrows that no smile could hide, and a sadness to his eyes that seemed to offset their crystalline color. Jimmy let go of his hand and stepped back. They stood momentarily looking each other up and down.

Cowboy made mental notes of the soft black leather shoes the reverend wore. They were beaten up and beyond repair. A pink stain blotched the tips of the reverend's left index and middle fingers. Next to his middle finger, the reverend was sporting a terribly tarnished silver wedding band. Both of the tips of his collar remained unbuttoned, likely because the left collar button was missing. His shirt was a rumpled blue pinstripe that was untucked on either side.

"Come have a seat," the reverend invited while guiding his guest to the padded floral chair at the front of his desk.

I'd love to, Cowboy thought, *if I could just see it*. Cowboy took half steps to the front of Reverend Bodean's desk and located the chair with his left kneecap. He sat cautiously in the deeply dented cushion, and having no other place to set his clipboard, he laid it in his lap and set his Stetson on top. Unlike Annabelle's desk, this one looked like it ate too much paper and threw up on itself.

Reverend Bodean sidestepped to the front of his overstuffed chair, grabbed it by the armrests, and seemed to scoot himself onto it and pull it under him in a single clumsy motion. Reverend

---

Bodean was not a very tall man, which required his adjustable chair to be set a little higher than average. He patted his hands across the mound of papers on his desk to inform Cowboy, "It's all right. I know exactly where everything is here."

Cowboy hung his hat on the arm of the chair and raised his clipboard. He held it at arm's length and slowly pulled it closer to his nose. The closer he pulled it to his face, the tighter the squint in his eyes became. As he continued to try focusing on his notes he began to explain, "There were just a few simple items I'd like to share with you regarding the boiler in the basement." Cowboy trailed off a little, then looked up at the reverend, who was leaning forward on his elbows trying desperately to look interested. "Do you mind if I put a little light on this?" Cowboy asked in the darkness.

"No. No. Not at all." Reverend Bodean smiled again as he reached up and tilted the beam of his desk lamp in Cowboy's direction.

"That's not exactly what I meant, sir." Cowboy rose from the dent and strolled toward the tightly shuttered windows. His thoughts were busily responding to the warning from the back of his mind as he unlatched the shutters. *Careful, hell*, he thought. *Asking permission is as careful as I know how to be.*

The first shutter seemed to explode open under the pressure of the sunlight that had been trying to pour into the office. Reverend Bodean visibly winced and squinted hard against the intrusion. The morning sun behind the second shutter seemed less intrusive as the pressure began to equalize in the room, and by the time Cowboy opened the third shutter to the church's backyard, the victorious daylight appeared bright and satisfied in its battle over the dark of Jimmy Bodean's office. Upon opening the last shutter, Cowboy looked over his right shoulder at the pale, squinting face of Reverend Bodean and asked, "Do you mind?"

Reverend Bodean naturally thought Cowboy was asking if he could keep the shutters open. "Of course. Of course," he told him. "I can't remember the last time those were open."

Cowboy threw open the third window with the view to the church's backyard and began purging the office of its sullen oppressiveness. "Wow!" he told the reverend. "What a beautiful day. It's gorgeous out there." He clomped across the wooden floor and dropped back into the dented cushion. On the way, Cowboy noted at least twenty dry vases scattered about the bookcases, the little coffee table near the far corner, the desk, the windowsills, and even on top of the bookcases, far higher than the good reverend could even reach.

As he sat back in his chair, he knew the vase on his desk was special. He caught the very slight aroma of the Issey Miyake perfume that the vase had been filled with when the rose was placed in it. The perfume is drawn up the stem of the flower, where it permeates and preserves the petals of the flowers, capturing the aroma. It was placed at the front of Reverend Bodean's desk near an old family photograph of a younger him, a stunning woman in her mid-thirties with long, shining, coal-black hair, and a small blond boy with a striped tee shirt and a delightful smile, sporting the same sea-blue eyes as the reverend. *Good-looking kid*, Cowboy thought as he raised his clipboard again and commenced his tedious oration.

"Yes. A beautiful day indeed," the reverend pretended to agree. "Now what was it you wanted to see me for?" Apparently, he found these things as tedious as Cowboy did.

"Well, there is a leaking flange on the water piping that you should get fixed before the snow starts flying around here. One thing about leaks is that they don't get better," Cowboy explained. The reverend found a slight smile for Cowboy's comment. "Once you fire up the boiler for heating this winter, you probably won't get another chance until late in the spring to fix it, unless of course it starts to leak so bad that you don't have any other choice. That'll make for some cold parishioners if you have to shut down to fix it come December."

That made them both smile a little easier. Cowboy felt that invading a man's space was not the best way to win friends, but there was never a space more in need of invading. The reverend's smile eased any remnant of anxiety that may have existed. He seemed to appreciate the matter-of-factness of Cowboy, and how he dulled the edges of seriousness at the same time.

"You may also want to start to budget for a chemical cleaning of the boiler and the heating system. This area has a lot of lime in the water, and you can see it building up around the leaking flange of the main water pipe," Cowboy continued. "You get that system cleaned, and in most cases, your heating bills can be cut in half."

"In half!" the reverend exclaimed. "How does that work?"

"Lime is a good insulator. If it's insulating your boiler and piping, it takes that much more fuel to heat the water and keep everyone warm," Cowboy explained. "Think of it like that scented rose on your desk there." He pointed toward the reverend's favorite flower with the tip of his pen. "Lime is drawn up through your hot water piping and into your radiators, clinging to the inside surfaces of the pipes all the way. The same way that Issey Miyake perfume was drawn up the stem of that rose so many years ago," he said, nodding at the vase at the front of the desk. "Here," he said, leaning his nose over the flower, "take a sniff and you can still smell it."

A gentle autumn breeze entered the rear window just then and carried the slight sweet smell of perfume to the reverend's nose. He sat there with a curious smile, staring at the flower and enjoying the smells the gust delivered. "You know, if you put a little water in there every once in a while, you'll be able to smell the perfume better. Of course, there's a tradeoff, because it won't hold the odor as long."

Cowboy could see that the reverend would start to well up if he didn't intercede. "Well," he announced, "that's about all I have for you. Let me write this stuff down for you so you won't forget."

The reverend's gaze averted to the tall figure sitting in front of him scribbling on a clipboard. "That's a good nose you got on you," he said. "I haven't smelled that perfume in a very long time."

"It comes with the territory," Cowboy offered. Jimmy was curiously peering at him with a half nervous smile.

"Careful now," the voice in the back of his mind nudged him again.

Yes, Cowboy thought back, *he's in an awful lot of pain.*

"Territory? What territory might that be?" the good reverend inquired with a smiling chuckle.

"Well, Reverend," Cowboy explained without looking up from his clipboard, "you might say I'm a professional noticer. I get paid to look all around machines when they break. I figure out how they work, how they break, and try to help people figure out how to fix them and keep them from breaking again. Over the years, I've just kind of developed a habit for noticing things."

"Seems you haven't limited yourself to just noticing machines," Jimmy observed with the same curious half smile.

"As I said," Cowboy replied with a single patient nod, "it comes with the territory."

"What else have you noticed around here?" Jimmy asked, with his own smile beginning to fade slightly.

Cowboy's pen froze. He looked across the desk at the reverend's curious faded smile. His eyes seemed to be pleading. The right corner of Cowboy's mouth turned slightly up into a sly grin that was barely recognizable. "Well," he started as he clutched his pen against the side of his metal clipboard, "I've noticed that you've got a build-up of lime in your pip..."

Jimmy cut him off. "Yes. You've mentioned that. What else have you noticed other than the boiler?" His smile widened a bit in unconvincing skepticism.

"Are you sure, Reverend?" Cowboy had a look of genuine concern on his face now, and the reverend recognized it.

"Sure," he said a little nervously, because he wasn't sure at all. "Go ahead and tell me what *you've noticed*." He had a healthy skepticism about him, but couldn't even pretend to be cynical, no matter how hard he tried. He leaned back in his big chair, set his elbows on the armrests, pressed his fingertips together, set his chin on his thumbs, and let the tips of his two index fingers come to rest directly under his nose in the little dent above his top lip. It was how he always posed himself to listen carefully, whether in a seminar or in counseling; this was how he sat to do nothing but listen.

Easy now...gently. The thought bounced off the back of Cowboy's mind.

I'll fire off a warning shot, he responded, *but I haven't got time for gentleness.*

"I need you to understand something first, Reverend," Cowboy began. "I'm not here to offend anyone or make anyone mad, although your secretary may have an element of disdain for me right about now. She's greatly concerned for you. She loves you deeply and feels a need to protect you, but hasn't got a clue how to go about it. Not knowing what else to do, she's taken on the role of your big sister. She takes that role very seriously, since it is all that she has; and you've been very gracious in allowing her to assume it, because it gives her comfort in these circumstances."

The reverend's eyes widened a little. "What circumstances might those be?" His voice seemed to soften a bit.

"That your beloved Rose died some five years ago, leaving you to finish raising your only child alone; that your seventeen-year-old son's girl problems are starting to hit real close to home; that the church is quickly dwindling; and that you both seem to be helpless to do anything at all about any of it."

"It was seven years ago," Jimmy responded. His voice had become very quiet; almost inaudible. His fingers quit their perching duties and were tightly laced together now, squeezing each other.

"Excuse me, sir?" Cowboy leaned in a little closer, hoping to hear better.

"She passed away seven years ago," he repeated through a small, restrained cough. Cowboy could just begin to see the reverend's sparkling blue eyes shine and moisten.

"Yes. Sorry. Seven years ago," Cowboy offered. "Would you like me to stop?"

Instead of whispering, the reverend unlocked his fingers long enough to twirl his left index in a "keep rolling" fashion, and interlaced them once again.

"You never really became bitter about any of it, and you're not depressed, but you are deeply saddened and have been for a long time. You gave the letters of Paul considerable scrutiny, but couldn't find any real comfort there. Lately, you've turned your attention to the Book of Ecclesiastes, in hopes to find some reason for it all. You're at a point now that you're wondering how such a depressing book ever made its way into the Bible. About the only comfort you manage to find in there are the passages read at your lovely bride's funeral. Funerals are one of those few occasions where the Book of Ecclesiastes is used almost exclusively."

"How do you know about my son?" Reverend Bodean whispered with his elbows pulled against his rib cage and his hands now tightly clutched to his chest.

"Sixteen is still a little too young for such nonsense in a small rural community. By eighteen, girl problems are practically encouraged. Seventeen seemed to fit closer to the date on your family photograph there too." Cowboy nodded to the picture beside the vase. "That, and the van. Ministry is not normally anywhere near the upper half of top earning careers, particularly small-town ministers. As such, the minister's kids are often stuck driving the family station wagon, or in your case, the van. Even though it looks pretty used up, it isn't beat up and wrecked. That might be expected if the boy were drinking and driving, so I wouldn't think he's terribly prone to getting intoxicated, in spite of any peer pressure he might be subjected to. No. The van is actually spotless. Even guys his age know that girls like to ride in cars that are clean, albeit a bit run down."

The reverend relaxed in his interest. "How do you know that I don't keep it clean like that?"

"Well, first of all, you don't have a girlfriend. If you did, you wouldn't be wandering around here in those beat-down, haggard shoes, wearing a shirt with collar buttons missing, and sporting that wedding band. The amount of tarnish on it would give some indication of how long ago your wife passed. Wives like to keep their husband's collar buttons sewn on, in good shoes, and above all, keep their wedding rings very polished and easily noticed."

"And my reading habits?" the reverend asked quietly.

"That's a bit of a stretch, I'll admit, but the Bible on your desk has dozens of Post-It notes hanging out and marking places near the beginning of the New Testament. Most of that part of the New Testament has Pauline authorship. I suspect you studied those pretty exclusively in your sadness. If you want to understand joy, it seems fitting to look for a man who found it in spite of spending thirteen years in a Roman prison. You figured if he could find it there, it can be found anywhere. At least, that's where I would have started looking anyway.

"The fun part is that there are no little pads of Post-It notes on your desk. You didn't find much help in Paul's letters, so you switched your attention to Ecclesiastes, which by most accounts is a most depressing piece of writing."

"Why aren't the Post-It notes in my desk?" Jimmy was starting to whisper again.

"What? Are you kidding me? There isn't anything in your desk. Everything is *on* your desk, including the empty cardboard backing of the last pad of Post-Its and the pink highlighter you've been using in Ecclesiastes just this morning." Cowboy nodded again at the right side of the mound of paper where the pink highlighter stood on its cap directly next to the vacant cardboard square. "Your Bible was opened to that book, and you have pink stains on the writing fingers of your left hand."

"I'm impressed," Reverend Bodean admitted, after relaxing and setting his elbows back on the armrests of his chair, although his hands were still tightly clutching each other. "Anything else?"

"Uh-huh. But this kind of noticing is pretty simple and concrete. The other stuff, what I call the deep noticing, gets a bit dodgy."

"What do you mean by deep noticing?"

"It's the kind where you only have experiential knowledge to go on. No solid evidence to support the conclusions, but you just know it 'cause you've seen it, or done it. It's something you just *know*," Cowboy repeated, lacking any better description.

"And what have you noticed so deeply?" Jimmy was truly curious now.

"Well, sir, do you think Paul was an exceptional person?" Cowboy's expression was one of anticipation.

"Of course. He expressed joy and an intention to do the Lord's work regardless of his circumstances." Jimmy's expression conveyed that he couldn't believe he was even asked such a silly question.

"Yes. He expressed a lot of things, and his letters to whoever their intended recipients were always start out describing his joy. Whether he was just beaten up and thrown out of the gates of Damascus, or locked up in prison again. He always expressed how joyful he was."

"Absolutely," Jimmy agreed. "He was an extraordinary man."

"In his letter to the Thessalonians he basically tells them, 'Look...I know you guys are going through some persecution there, but can you really complain? I mean really, look at all I've endured for our cause. I've been beaten, stoned, imprisoned, sacrificed a pretty cushy lifestyle, and I still have this tremendous joy. Can you guys really complain about a few harsh comments from the local government?' Of course, I'm paraphrasing, but that's the gist of what he's telling them." Cowboy looked at the reverend, wondering if he would concede.

"Well, okay. Yes. That is basically what he is telling them," the reverend agreed.

"Now I don't know about you, but I'm pretty sure that I could not be joyful with people beating me up, locking me in prison, feeding me a bowl of swill a day, or losing the soft bed, hot showers, and freedoms I enjoy daily. Again, that's just me, but could you do it?"

"No. I don't think so. But that's what makes Paul so exceptional."

"Exactly, and it is also what gives us a great excuse. Paul could do it, but, by his own accounts, he was exceptional. I can't do it. I'm not as tough, or as smart, or as faithful, or as connected as Paul was. Compared to Paul, I am in no way exceptional, so I shouldn't be expected to offer such an exceptional response in the midst of misery." Cowboy spoke quietly, and held his hands out on either side as if preparing to throw a pizza dough. "Listen, I don't want to take anything away from Paul. He was a tough man born in tough times. He was driven to make a decision and he stuck to it."

"No. No. Go ahead. This is interesting," Jimmy encouraged.

Cowboy leaned forward and uncovered a Rubik's cube half buried under the heap on Jimmy's desk. "May I?"

"Please do. Every blue moon when my desk is clear, I find that silly thing and work on it until I'm nearly blind. Have at it."

"Well, you couldn't find any comfort in Paul's letters because he gave us a great excuse. He was special and we just don't much feel that way about ourselves lately. So, let's talk about Solomon for a minute, and that Book of Ecclesiastes you've been poring over lately. Take a look at this puzzle." Cowboy brought the Rubik's cube up to eye level, resting his right elbow on a bare spot on Jimmy's desk. "How many sides does this thing have?"

"It has six," Jimmy said, sitting up a little closer.

"How many can you see?"

"I can only see three sides."

"You see," Cowboy began turning the puzzle, spinning it by its corners between the tips of his long middle finger and his thumb and flicking it with his ring finger, "every time you turn the little row or column, it not only has an impact on the three sides you can see, it also has an effect on those three you cannot see. It is the predicting of the impact on the sides you cannot see that makes the puzzle so difficult. Have you got the instructions to this thing?"

"No. I picked it up probably five years ago. I didn't lose the directions. I threw them out," Reverend Bodean stated with a chuckle. "At the time, I guess I figured it was cheating to use the instructions. I mean, anyone can follow instructions...can't they?" Jimmy's expression showed justification when he admitted this.

"Over a quadrillion different combinations, and only one solution." Cowboy's mouth turned up again into his sly little half smile. "And you only see half of what you are doing. Did you ever solve it?"

"Oh, heck no." Jimmy chortled. "I can only ever get one side to come out."

Cowboy removed the Stetson and clipboard from his lap and laid them on the floor next to his chair. He placed the puzzle on the edge of Reverend Bodean's desk and, after unbuttoning the cuffs of his starched and pressed snow-white shirt, he rolled the sleeves up to his elbows. He plucked the puzzle back off Jimmy's desk, studied it for a moment, then hung it in his right hand beside the arm of his chair. "Solomon was a very sharp nut," he continued. "He's probably the masochist that invented the silly thing. If he were doing this puzzle, he would not only consider how every turn of the little columns and rows affected the sides of the puzzle he could see, but he would also understand exactly how each of those turns impacted the half of the puzzle he could not see."

Cowboy leaned back far into the chair, giving Jimmy permission to do the same as they relaxed. "You've been a practicing theologian for how long now?" he asked.

"Twenty-two years."

"Tell me who wrote the Book of Ecclesiastes."

"Well," Jimmy sat a little straighter, now that they were in his realm of expertise, "there's a lot of debate over that. Some scholars think it was dictated by Solomon to a scribe, or even written much later by someone who heard or transcribed the pages that Solomon wrote."

"Why would they think that?" Cowboy asked, seeing that Jimmy was starting to enjoy this conversation.

"It's because it is written in third person. It starts out with the words 'So says the Teacher, the son of David.'" Reverend Bodean was looking around the office now, trying to identify a strange clicking noise.

"What do you think?" Cowboy asked.

"Oh, I don't know. I suspect it was actually transcribed by someone else," Reverend Bodean answered, still looking for the strange noise.

"What does it say next?"

Reverend Bodean's eyes returned to Cowboy to answer his question. He identified Cowboy as the source of the clicking noise.

He had put his hands together behind the chair and was turning the little rows and columns of the Rubik's cube between them. Cowboy now sat with his right ankle on his left knee, looking directly at him. Reverend Bodean's voice was beginning to soften again. "It says 'Vanity, Vanity, Vanity...all I see is vanity.'"

"That's right," Cowboy confirmed, with the clicking droning on behind him. "Unless you read a more modern translation that says it's meaningless, meaningless, meaningless. The book goes on to tell us that there is nothing new under the sun. Whatever you are doing has been done before. There is a season for everything; a season to sew; a season to reap; a time to laugh and a time to cry. It tells us that there is no advantage to being rich and even the stillborn are better off, because they never got to know the difference." Reverend Bodean was solidly fixed on Cowboy now. His hands found each other and began clutching at his chest again. "It is basically telling us that Solomon was the richest person on the earth and he still found no satisfaction, despite giving his heart everything it desired. He says you won't find anything of any interest at all under the sun. But then," Cowboy paused, but the clicking continued, "it says something like 'the only thing you can really hope for is to find joy in what you do, for that is your lot in life.'"

"Yes," Reverend Bodean whispered.

Cowboy dropped his right leg back on the floor and sat up a little straighter. "Can you see how utterly simple it is? Can you hear Solomon saying, *Who cares?*" Cowboy enunciated the words very carefully. "Who cares? Who cares if you're rich? Chances are your kids will turn out spoiled rotten and when you die, these selfish little fools are going to get all your money without ever turning a wrench to earn it. Right? So, who cares if you're rich?"

Cowboy was smiling widely now. "Who cares if you're poor or sick? There is a season for everything, and seasons come and they go. There's nothing new under the sun, so who cares?" Cowboy was almost laughing now. "Don't you find that somehow liberating? Solomon saying it doesn't matter if you're a king or a pauper. It doesn't matter if you're rich or poor. Love and hate; hope and sadness and money come and go and the only thing you can really hope for is to find joy in what you do, whether it's sweep the streets, manage a business, or perform brain surgery." Cowboy was almost giggling at this point, even with the annoying clicking sound echoing off the back of his chair. "Solomon says, 'Look, I thought that joy was about the material things and so I denied my heart nothing. That didn't work at all. I thought it was about wisdom so I ran to get me some of that, and found I was chasing the wind. It turns out, folks, that it isn't about what you have; it's about what you *do*. And what you do is irrelevant, as long as you find joy in it.'"

"You see," Cowboy was deepening his thoughtfulness and softening his smile, "Solomon was a bit of a puzzler himself. He knew that he couldn't just tell what would bring us joy, because joy is something that has to be chosen in whatever it is we find ourselves doing. We aren't going to find it in our brilliance, or earnings statement, or money, or sex, or drugs. We can only find it in what we do, regardless of what that may be; help the old lady cross the street, help a guy fix his flat tire in the rain, buy ice cream for the family in front of you at the Baskin-Robbins. He appears to write it in such a depressing manner, hoping that when you read it, you are able to see the depression we all face at some point, and think beyond it. He doesn't really use any depressing words, but it is certainly the tone conveyed there.

"And that is the easy side of Solomon's puzzle, those three sides of it you can see," Cowboy added. "The hard sides of this enigma are the ones you can't see. He also knew that he couldn't take credit for saying it."

Reverend Bodean's elbows were clamped against his rib cage. "Why's that?" he whispered.

"It would have given us the same excuse that Paul gave us. It would be too easy for us to say 'Well, sure, Sol. All of this is great stuff coming from the king of the earth and the richest man that ever lived.' He knew that if we had an excuse, we would use it. I'm not exceptional. I'm not wealthy and in charge. I'm pretty sure that Solomon wrote the book. I'm pretty sure he wrote it in third person on purpose. Solomon was a sharp nut," Cowboy told him while gently setting the solved Rubik's Cube on the corner of his desk. "And if he would have signed this book he knew how it would have impacted the sides of the puzzle you can't see. He knew that it would have allowed us to excuse it as nothing more than vanity, vanity vanity; and likely render the entire thing meaningless, meaningless, meaningless to us poor mooks reading it."

Reverend Bodean sat staring at the solved Rubik's Cube with his mouth a little agape. He slowly raised his eyes toward Cowboy, causing the tear that had welled up to release and slither around the apple of his right cheek.

"Paul was basically telling us, 'I am exceptional because I found joy in spite of what was done to me,'" Cowboy summarized. "Solómon is telling us, 'No one is any more exceptional than anyone else and we can all find joy in what we happen to be doing.' Now, sir," Cowboy tilted the Rubik's Cube onto one corner and spun it like a top, "if there are over a quadrillion combinations and only one solution to finding joy, I would read the instructions, cheat, give up everything, or acquire whatever was necessary to find that solution for my life."

"B-but my wife is gone," Jimmy quietly stammered. "How am I supposed to find joy in that?" The puzzle clattered back to the desktop.

"You have to think about the sides of the puzzle you cannot see; perhaps from your late wife's perspective." The puzzle on Reverend Bodean's desk stared back at him. "Solomon suggests that we find joy in what we do, for that is our lot in life. He does not suggest that we find misery in all that we cannot do. Your wife is gone. That is your lot in life. Should you find misery because you will never again take her to the street dance, or out for ice cream and a movie? Those are things you cannot do anymore."

The reverend, of course, knew this, but hearing it spoken out loud was more painful than he thought it would be. A tear now streamed around the left apple of his cheek. "No," he whispered in agonizing agreement.

"Imagine the impact you are having on the sides of this puzzle you cannot see. It seems most likely that one of you had to die first. I look around this room and can spot over twenty little items in memoriam of your lovely Rose. You loved her deeply and know the pain of being stuck on this miserable planet without her." Cowboy's eyes softened even more now. "If she loved you even half as much, then you can imagine the pain she was spared by not outliving you. What if she loved you even more? Try to find comfort in knowing she was spared the pain that you are enduring. *Doing* that may help you find joy again. *Not* doing that leaves you to the mercy of Paul's exceptionalness, and finding joy in spite of your lot in life. That's a tougher nut to crack because it doesn't require you to *do* anything, only that you must *be* exceptional.

"Another thing that you can *do* is take your son out for ice cream and a movie, or a ball game, or a tractor pull, or a rock concert, or fishing, or take up karate, rebuild that van, or whatever you two come up with. In *doing* that, you may actually start to feel the inklings of joy creeping back into your life. Perhaps one day, in *doing* those things with his children, you may even find yourself overjoyed. The problem is, if you don't do it with him, chances are you will not do it with your lovely bride's grandchildren."

That was the tap that opened the tear ducts on the good reverend. Although he was not crying exactly, he was quickly panting and wiping his face on his shirt sleeve.

"Well," Cowboy muttered while reaching for his clipboard and hat, "what the hell do I know? I'm just a dumb town kid from Wyoming."

He tore the perforation on the top piece of paper clamped to the metal clipboard and aligned its corners with the paper his notes were written on. He slipped a business card that was hiding behind the snuff can in his shirt pocket on top of the papers, and punched the top of the stapler on the left edge of the reverend's desk to join them. As Cowboy did this, Reverend Bodean took the time to gather himself.

"Well, Reverend," Cowboy started while handing him the paperwork, "it has been a real pleasure meeting you."

"Th-the pleasure has been all mine," he whispered, taking the documents with his left hand and offering his right to the tall, lean figure in front of him.

Cowboy took his hand deeply and, with a saddened look into the reverend's eyes, told him, "I am sorry about your lovely wife, sir. I am sorry that such a good man seems to have pulled such a sorrowful lot." The reverend knew that Cowboy's sincerity was genuine. And with his sly little half smile, he added, "And I don't think your secretary much cares for me."

"She loved Rose too," the reverend told him. "I wouldn't be too offended."

"I never am." Cowboy smiled freely, until the phone on Jimmy's desk rudely interjected.

"Bbbbbrrrrriiiiinnnnngggg, BBBBBRRRRRIIIIIINNNNNGGGG," it insisted, seeming to get louder.

3

THE YOUNG SEMINARIAN

I.

"**B**BBBRRRRRIIIINNNNGG!" Cowboy's desk phone erupted, jerking him out of his reverie. His memory of
Revered Bodean so rudely interrupted caused him to
jump, raising his heavy Double H riding boots off the corner of his
desk and throwing his right hand toward the phone.

The earth froze when, in the perfect inverted pike position, Cowboy realized that his desk chair creaked toward obliv-
ion and the possibility of overbalancing became very real.
"BBBBBRRRRRIIIINNNNGGG!" The blast from the second ring
seemed to decide the outcome of these precarious acrobatics, and
a deep nervous laugh began welling up in Cowboy's psyche. Before
the laugh found its way to his throat, he yelled, "Doorstop!" in a
single, loud note to no one. Just a week before, the city tore the
street up in front of Cowboy's house. It was originally constructed of brick. The city managed to tear several up last winter with a
snowplow, and the mayor vowed to have it paved before snow flew
again.

While ripping up the old brick, Cowboy collected one to use for
a doorstop. It so happened that this morning, when he took the
trash to the curb, Cowboy propped the front door open with the

brick to welcome the smell of autumn into the office area he used just off the front entry. It also happened that he did not kick the brick back against the wall when he closed the door, and there it lay directly behind his chair double-dog-daring the pending disaster to just go ahead and ensue.

Cowboy could not be sure where he was in relation to the brick doorstop, but three thoughts fired through his mind when the ringing phone shoved noisily at him. "You have got to be kidding me... This could really hurt." And, "I'll probably choke on my Copenhagen."

This third thought actually stirred a mild panic in him, and as his chair edged over the cliff of ridiculousness, Cowboy used his tongue to deftly scoop the tobacco from his cheek and hacked the cud in a long arch over his boots. The only thing left to do was laugh, which he did as he spoke aloud. "You dirty rat bast..." WHUMP!

The exact point where his head was attached to his neck landed flush on the flat of the brick. Saliva stained the color of tobacco shot straight up from his open mouth, and just before losing consciousness, Cowboy could feel the inside of his mouth instantly numb.

II.

The cool marble felt incredibly good against my naked back when I awoke on the floor. I rolled over wearing nothing but surgical scrub pants, dark blue, with a drawstring for a belt, and lay my cheek against the stone coolness like a drunk leaning against a toilet bowl. There was a single ass pocket and I could feel the familiar round tin of Copenhagen loosely stuffed in it when I sat up, rolling to my left hip and reaching for the goose egg growing on the back of my head.

I stood slowly. *Damn! That's really going to hurt!* As I ascended to my feet, I could feel the sensation returning in my mouth, now filled with the metallic sweetness of blood. I verified that I was not bleeding and the coppery taste was only the nerves firing in my tongue again. I shook the darkness off my vision when the room once again tried to grow black; the light stretching away from me down a long circular corridor and snapping back into full view upon shaking my head for a second time with added vigor.

Why has He got me here again? What did I do now? The questions fired through my fogged consciousness without even slowing for consideration. It felt like I was in junior high school again as I looked down the long, marble hallway that led to the glimmering arched doors that had every appearance of some sort of principal's office. I had seen these doors before on several occasions. Opening them always brought me into His study-slash-library-slash-laboratory. I was never very certain what the room might have been called, but it contained countless books, and there were microscopes and test tubes and Bunsen burners and scales of all kinds found directly behind the enormous rolltop desk.

I opened the door and watched Him for a moment. He rolled His padded stool from the desk to the long lab table behind it and adjusted the bright blue flame under a large beaker. The collection of steam at the top of the beaker increased and flowed down a coiled glass tube, over a cooler, and dripped condensate into a scaled flask. He was purifying something, but I had no idea what it could have been. The liquid being vaporized at the front end of the process was as black as road tar, but the condensate dripping into the flask was so clear, I had to squint to see the level in the flask jump with each new drop of liquid entering.

He rolled back to His desk and, without looking up, reached for a large book that wasn't there the first time I looked. He pulled the book down onto the writing surface of His desk and flipped it open near the center pages and plainly ordered, "Take three of those ibuprofen in your medicine cabinet when you get back. It'll take the edge off that knot on your noodle."

"Yeah," I told Him. "And thanks for that. You know you could have just texted me, paged me over the loudspeaker at the airport, or even spoken to me through the neighbor's dog. There was really no need to be so subtle as to render me unconscious on the office floor with a throat full of snoose juice."

"Ah! That reminds me." He began to quickly poke the top corner of His rolltop desk with His index finger until an audible thumping emerged, indicating that whatever I was about to give Him was to be placed right there. "You owe me."

I didn't even have to ask. Every time I came to Him it seemed to require some form of payment, but that does not accurately describe the conditions of this unspoken agreement. This was more of an exchange of one aspect of myself for an aspect of His. I had discovered that those aspects of His, those perspectives and revelations that burrowed into the tidy package I had wrapped the world within, often served to alienate me from it.

"What do you mean I owe you? I didn't call this meeting. You did." I immediately realized what a ridiculous question it was. Of course, I owed Him. I owed Him everything...and all of me. The entire universe was His and I happened to be a part of it. He watched the panic fill my eyes as I suddenly recognized that all I had at that moment was a pair of surgical scrub pants and a can of Copenhagen, and He knew I was not going to give up my pants. The thought of my pants brought the clarity that if everything is His, then **everything** is His. I was His. I was in His study, wearing His pants and carrying His Copenhagen. Every time I had been here before it felt as if I was asked to give something up. During this encounter I came to understand that I had never given anything up, but given it back. I couldn't give Him what was His all along.

I slipped my fingers into the rear pocket of the scrubs and slowly pulled the tin out, placing it on the spot He had now stopped tapping on the top corner of His beautifully engraved desk. As soon as I had placed the can onto the dark, rich wood, it began dissolving into the desk. He reached over and held my left cheek in the warm palm of His right hand. "And thank you for that," He said with a smiling sadness. It felt like an expression my mother would often get when comforting me through some minor illness or injury. It was soft, unworried, and aware of the pain.

I closed my eyes and tried to get lost in the warmth of His hand. "I've got a project I need your help with." When He spoke while His hands were on me, every word had a color and texture that rippled through the fabric of me. It caused me to pulse and hum loud and deep until the sound from within magnified and amplified my consciousness. It felt like an orgasmic heightening of terror and awareness, ever escalating, expanding me to an intimate subatomic knowledge of everything that I am.

This must be what Superman feels like, I thought above this blissful fear threatening to push me to an indestructible implosion.

"To me, you are Superman," He answered my thought while pulling His hand from my cheek, forcing my eyes to snap open, "and I need you to suit up."

"What have you got in mind for me? Another chance encounter that rips the grip of stability from the grasp of an innocent bystander?"

"Yes. Something like that, but you already know that I don't much allow bystanding, innocent or otherwise." He smiled slyly. "And this isn't about you offering an alternative perspective that keeps an innocent man awake at nights with nothing better to think about. This is about My setting the course of someone's path; bringing them to a clearer understanding of divine purpose."

"And what divine purpose might that be?" I asked with more interest than I truly had in the answer.

"Soon," He answered simply and straightforward. Then He began running His fingers through my hair as a reminder of the three He sent so many years ago, and the impact that they had in my life. He leaned into my ear and whispered while combing my hair back, "Remember the truth I gave you when you asked Me how to reconcile your spiritual conflict." As He did this, the overwhelming Superman feeling washed over me in waves again.

"I remember. I also remember how long I struggled and fought under that truth. Do I have to go?"

"I'm afraid so, My boy," He replied. "But if you continue to listen, you will have no need to miss Me, nor I you."

Before I started the walk back down the marble corridor, I looked into His oceanic eyes and said, "I'm going to miss the Copenhagen."

He pulled open one of the hundreds of little cubby drawers that filled the back of His magnificent desk and dipped the long middle finger of His right hand into the creamy gray dust inside the drawer. He reached His left hand behind my head and gently cupped the back of my neck, deftly reaching up and touching His freshly dusted middle finger directly between my eyebrows, forcing the lids to slowly draw sedately closed. "No, you won't," He promised.

A bell rang behind Him in an antique ringtone sound: DING-A-LING...DING-A-LING. "Ah," He announced. "It's ready." He spun around and turned the burner off the black tar substance He had been distilling.

III.

DING-A-LING...DING-A-LING. The cell phone clipped to his belt rang its antique ringtone, causing Cowboy to lurch, heaving his chest off the office floor, hacking and choking up remnants of Copenhagen that lodged in his throat during his most recent stupidity. "Oh! You son-of-a-DING-A-LING!" He could tell by the ringtone assigned that it was Mike, so Cowboy did not let it ring a third time before answering.

He slipped the phone out of its holster and through one squinted eye recognized the "answer" button on the touch screen. Punching it and drawing the phone to his ear, Cowboy answered, "What's up, Chief?"

"What the hell you doing, man? Still sleeping?" Mike sounded bright as the autumn sunrise.

"Sort of." Cowboy managed a wry smirk in spite of the pounding that was building up behind his eyes. He had pulled himself to his feet by then and was lumbering toward the bathroom holding his eyes in their sockets with the thumb and middle finger of his left hand.

"Well, shake loose. We got work to do. I need you to get down to GE's heavy frame shop in Houston as quick as you can. There's a 7FA that arrived there two days ago from Taiwan and they've asked us to do a damage assessment. We need to get there when they open the casing to figure out what caused the wreck."

Cowboy retrieved the extra-strength ibuprofen, shook three of them out onto the edge of the sink, and stood looking at himself in the mirror while filling up his rinsing cup with cold tap water. There was a perfect drop of tobacco-stained saliva that had landed in a familiar way immediately between his eyebrows. *Gross!* he thought to his mirrored image.

He first rinsed the tobacco out of his mouth and throat before answering Mike. "I can take off on the direct flight later this morning and be in Houston by about two o'clock this afternoon. Have you got a job number?" Cowboy glugged down the tablets with the mouthful of water that was left in the cup.

"Eleven one eighty-six," Mike answered. "This is really great. I really appreciate you doing this." Mike's appreciation was infectious. It was Cowboy's favorite quality in him because it was genuine.

"I'll let you know how it goes once I get there and meet up with the shop foreman. Is Buster still running that place?"

"You bet," Mike answered, "and I've already warned him that you're headed his way."

Cowboy chuckled. "It never fails to make me laugh when you ask me to do the job already knowing that I will. It would seem more efficient if you just called up and said, 'Go to Houston. Buster is expecting you.'" Cowboy laughed out loud now.

"Oh. Well, I didn't want you to feel left out of the process, but I'll keep that in mind." Mike was laughing now.

"All right, Colonel," Cowboy finished. "If I'm going to make this morning's flight I've got to get Christy on the phone. We'll talk soon."

"You bet." Mike hung up the phone.

Cowboy thought about this part of his consulting work as he brushed his teeth. His head was thumping now instead of pounding, so the ibuprofen had started to kick into gear. The pain could be easily felt but his thoughts were not hiding in it. Something about this part of his work energized him. It was the way that whatever he was doing, no matter what it might be, had to be dropped and he had to get everything rolling in the right direction to make sure the project was ready for him on the other side of the country, or the other side of the world.

That's why he called Christy "Angel." This young lady worked for a travel agency and she made it her daily ambition to ensure that Cowboy's trips were as uneventful as possible. She seemed to know everything about every airline, every flight, and every destination that Cowboy might be preparing to travel to, including hotels, ground transportation, and, if time permitted, any fun or interesting things to look into while there. The one thing about Christy was that she personalized this knowledge specifically for Cowboy's taste to the point that all he had to do was call her and say, "Houston...today...ASAP...returning tonight late." He wouldn't even have to tell her who it was, and within five minutes the itinerary would be landing in his inbox.

Cowboy was fascinated with this woman's ability. The only time he ever recognized a moment's hesitation was when he called her up and told her he had to get to Pekanbaru, Sumatra. "I don't even know where Sumatra is," she admitted. "Where the heck is Pekanbaru?" She laughed loudly. Within ten minutes she called and told Cowboy that it was a good thing he liked coffee, 'cause this trip was going to be a little slice of heaven.

Her phone rang one and a half times. "Good morning," she chimed. "Where are we headed today?"

"Houston. I need to get there an hour ago and need to be back tonight. Can you make that happen?" he asked, already knowing the answer.

"Well...let's see here. You be on that ten-thirty flight and I can get you back on the seven-fifty out of Houston Hobby if that gives you enough time. No hotel, but do you need a car?"

"Sounds exactly right," Cowboy agreed, "and I will need a car. Whatever rental agency suits you."

"You start driving and I'll send the confirmations. Have a safe trip."

Cowboy hung up the phone and lifted his travel pack off the hook on the side of his bookcase. He shut down his laptop and threw it, his digital camera, and his travel wallet into the pack and rolled his Dodge Ram over the ninety-minute drive to the airport. He missed the Ranger because it was lighter and got better gas mileage, but his one-ton was powerful enough to pull his trailered horses. Before he crossed the edge of the city limits, he heard the distinct chirping bird ringtone he assigned Christy's contact information, signifying the confirmations had landed in his inbox.

As usual, their timing was impeccable. Cowboy parked his truck, walked to the terminal, disassembled and re-assembled his brief packings through security, and strolled to his departure gate. There were no unforeseen wrecks on the highway, stalling road construction, or idling trains to throw the plan out of whack. He handed the agent his boarding pass upon arrival at the gate, took his seat, and enjoyed a nap on the two-hour and fifteen-minute flight to Houston. The whole thing was glitchless.

IV.

Cowboy was more tired than he realized. It may have been the harried trip to the airport or the head thumping he took earlier that morning, but the next thing that came to his realization was the landing gear clunking and whining into place as the plane approached its landing in Houston. Grabbing his rucksack and stretching his legs toward the ground transportation area on the lower level of the airport, he winced at the sore reminder of the goose egg on the back of his head when dropping his hat into place.

Angel had a rental car waiting for him, and the traffic around the outer beltway had cleared to a steady rate by the time Cowboy started his thirty-five-minute drive to the shop where Buster was sipping a cup of stale coffee and stabbing his tongue at the remnants of his chicken salad lunch that lodged between two molars. Cowboy knew Buster was an old hand and would make his visit as short and as efficient as possible. The hot coffee, the nap on the plane, and the warm weather had Cowboy feeling much better when he strode into Buster's office.

"Mornin," Cowboy offered with a smile as he took Buster's hand and shook it one time definitively. "How the heck have you been?"

"Great. Just great," Buster replied. "Finally got that last daughter married off to a really nice kid. I'll never know what he sees in her." Buster laughed. "She's as tough and mean as a rattlesnake!"

"Little Connie is married?! How the heck did that girl grow up so fast? Congratulations, Buster. Really, that's fantastic!" Cowboy slapped him on the shoulder blade with sincerity. "My word, where did the time go?" Buster's eyes were drifting toward a distant memory when Cowboy reeled him back in. "You cried at the wedding, didn't you?" Cowboy's wide smile at the suggestion assured Buster that it was perfectly all right if he did cry at his own daughter's wedding.

"Damn right I cried!" Buster smiled right back. "Do you have any idea how much a wedding costs? I'm going to be stuck here catering to the likes of old rednecks like you for another dozen years just to get back to an even bank balance." That made Cowboy laugh out loud. "Speaking of which, we'd better get you out on the shop floor to look at this thing before the boys start tearing it apart. Come on. I'll go with you," and he led Cowboy out of his office toward the gas turbine rotor that waited for them in the far corner of the enormous shop floor.

The next three hours were filled with getting the backstory on the engine and reviewing the machine's history and sequence of events that brought it to this point. Any gaps in the technical queries were filled with playful jibes and small talk, and true to form, Buster had Cowboy walking back through the front doors and on his way in plenty of time to refuel and return the car and catch his 7:50 p.m. flight out of Houston's Hobby Airport.

By the time he cleared security and boarded the plane, his headache was starting to well up behind his eyes again. He took three more of the ibuprofen he pocketed before leaving home and was looking forward to his return nap as he dropped into the aisle seat next to a very young Christian man. *More like a boy*, Cowboy thought as he looked over the fellow. Sandals, short, dark hair neatly trimmed over the ears, dark eyes, and a silver cross studded into his left earlobe, he was wearing a black T-shirt with a figure of a white cross streak-painted on the chest.

Cowboy's nose told him that the young man's clothes had been freshly laundered. The single half-empty backpack in the overhead compartment, and the toothbrush and New Testament in the seat pocket in front of him led Cowboy to the conclusion that his young travel companion was home for a short stay. No one could make clothes smell like that except Momma. "What year of seminary are you in?" Cowboy inquired as the seat back creaked against his re-laxing slump.

"How did you know I was in seminary?"

The look of surprise on the young man's face left Cowboy struggling with the image of anyone calling this man-child "Father."

"It wasn't too terribly difficult to figure that one out, Jason," Cowboy answered to an even deeper look of amazement. He held out his hand. "Most folks call me Cowboy."

Jason slowly placed his hand in Cowboy's as an automatic, robotic response to all of the hands he had ever shaken in his life. Cowboy snapped it up and shook it firmly, thinking the whole time that the young fellow's limp hand felt more like a warm fish. "Nice to meet you," Cowboy said in a manner that would lead Jason to believe that he really thought it was nice to meet him.

"It's the smell of Bounce fabric softener on your clothes that your momma just pulled from the dryer before you left for the airport this evening." Cowboy decided to let the kid off the hook before his chin wore a hole in the crucifix of that T-shirt. "The crucifix on your shirt, the one hanging on that chain around your neck, and the one pinned to your earlobe, along with the New Testament you've been reading. Then there's the Creighton University duffle with your name tag on it," Cowboy offered, poking his thumb toward the overhead luggage bin where the young man's modest weekend travel tote was stored. "So, what year are you in?"

"Second semester of my first year," Jason answered, still a little stunned.

"Don't think too much of it," Cowboy said, sincerely. "It's a lot of observation and very little magic. Mind if I ask why you've chosen this particular career path? You must be absolutely brilliant and fully committed to have been accepted to such a prestigious private university." Cowboy knew that the best way to get young people to talk was to make them the topic of discussion.

Jason beamed. "Well, I've been involved in my church my whole life and have gotten a lot of support from them, so there are some deep roots there. Plus, I think my mother really wanted me to attend a Catholic school."

"All good answers, but not really for the question I asked. Why did you choose this particular career path? I understand why the church would have wanted you there, and every young man's mother wants them to enter a path of ministry, but why did you choose this path?"

"Hmmmm..." Jason paused. "That answer usually suffices for most of the people who have asked. I guess I could tell you how I have been chosen, or that a great calling has come over me, or I've been assigned a great commission, but I don't know that any of those things have actually happened in such a dramatic way. I guess it just comes down to my belief. I believe in God, that the church is a good cause, and committing myself to its purpose and sharing my belief with others is a task everyone should commit to," Jason offered.

Cowboy chuckled softly. "You've definitely chosen a career path that will put that commitment to the test. It is filled with persecution, under constant scrutiny, encourages poverty, and often rejects common sense." Cowboy's expression faded into a contemplative seriousness at the completion of his thoughts. "Yours is a career that continuously flourishes as you continuously surrender and will force you to find the end of yourself on a daily basis."

"That sounds dismal."

"Unless, of course, your joy lies only within your faith and your task is only to find the truth." Cowboy's expression lightened. "Then all that comes with it is only designed to demonstrate your faith and expose the truth. Does that make sense?"

There was a swollen pause as Jason contemplated what Cowboy had just told him. "Yes," he announced, after catching hold of Cowboy's thought. "I think I see what you're saying. A commitment to faith and truth is a burden too heavy for anyone to carry. The only relief anyone carrying it could hope for is the joy found in obtaining a deeper faith and discovering a deeper truth, which comes from the constant persecution and scrutiny." Jason smiled a little. "Bit of a predicament. Kind of a masochistic approach, don't you think?"

"Yup. It's also kind of the truth. It's even a notion that is biblically supported. *Consider it pure joy, my brothers...*"

"*When faced with troubles of many kinds,*" Jason finished. "James chapter one, verse two." He smiled.

Cowboy turned his head and offered Jason a deep nod of approval. He was impressed with this young man. "*Blessed are they which are persecuted for righteousness' sake...*"

"*For theirs is the kingdom of heaven,*" Jason finished for him. "I think that's in Matthew somewhere." He rolled his eyes looking for the specific reference but couldn't find it. "*For to you it is given in the behalf of Christ, not only to believe in him...*"

"*But to suffer for his sake.*" Cowboy had a little awe smeared across his own face at this point. "In the letters of Paul to the Philippians. Terribly impressive."

Jason smiled back at him. "I grew up in the church. My mom was a single parent and I'm sure she found a lot of security for me there, so when she wasn't working and I wasn't in school, we were studying the Bible, memorizing verses and involved in church activities. It's really all we did while I was growing up aside from the occasional trip to the zoo or movie." There was another long pause while Cowboy's imagination brought up clips of a young woman in Texas. With Jason's dark hair and dark eyes, she might have been Mexican or Latino, but the hair and eyes were the only genetic traits Jason inherited. The slight build, pale skin, and very light splatter of freckles across his nose all appeared to be more Anglican.

"Mind if I ask you a question?" Jason broke the pause.

"By all means," Cowboy insisted, "ask away."

"You mentioned earlier that this profession often rejects common sense. What did you mean by that?"

He really is listening, Cowboy thought, and the next idea that bounced off the back of his mind insisted, *Best be careful what you say, then*. Cowboy rolled the words cautiously in his mouth before opening it. "I simply meant that there are biblical stories that defy common sense, and you may find yourself in a position one day where you might have to explain the lapse in logic. In fact, some might find the very premise of good and evil, or God and Satan, a contradiction in logic. It can be a daunting task, not only to work others through those contradictions, but to work yourself through them."

There was another long pause before Cowboy asked, "Surely within the knowledge you've amassed you have come across what you might consider a contradiction in logic. Can you give me any examples?"

"Well," Jason hesitated. "There is the story of Abraham, which I've always thought was a bit of a contradiction."

"How so?"

"You of course know the story of God commanding Abraham to take his favorite son, Isaac, into the wilderness and offer him as a sacrifice."

"Yes. A story of incredible faith. Walking for two days, trying to sort through God's promise to Abraham that Isaac would be the father of nations, and then being asked to kill him. Must have been a long two days' walk out into the wilderness knowing that only one of them would be making the walk back." Cowboy nodded. "A good story, but where is the contradiction?"

"If you read the whole story of Abraham, when he was previously trekking through the wilderness, he came across three travelers on their way to destroy Sodom and Gomorrah. Upon learning of their intentions, he began to negotiate with the travelers to spare the city."

"That's right," Cowboy recalled. "Genesis reported that *if I find fifty righteous people in Sodom, I will spare the whole place for their sake.* Oh," he added with some astonishment, "it never occurred to me that a man of unwavering faith; a faith so strong that he is willing to sacrifice his favorite child; a young child, pure and innocent and good." Cowboy smiled slightly at the insight offered by this brilliant young fellow.

"Yeah. See?" Jason said. "How is it that a man with this unwavering faith, who does not question God's order to sacrifice his innocent son, come to negotiate for a city of strangers filled with sin?"

"Excellent point of contradiction," Cowboy replied. "I'm not sure. I hadn't taken any note of it until now. You know," he added, "Lot and his family lived there at the time, and if I remember correctly, the two were related somehow."

"Lot was Abraham's nephew," Jason told him.

"Well, did you come to understand why there is this contradiction in the story?"

"I can't be sure, but I suspect it's to show how a man's faith can grow, and a man of faith can get what he requests of God. While God inevitably did what He set out to do and Sodom and Gomorrah was destroyed, Lot's family...well...most of his family, was spared from the destruction. While He told Abraham to sacrifice Isaac, He also spared Abraham the loss."

"Oh, I see what you're saying. Abraham's faith grew in his relationship with God until he reached the point of demonstrating a willingness to sacrifice Isaac. Very clever." *This kid is smart. I'd attend his sermons*, Cowboy thought.

"I think so," Jason added. "I think it is to remind us that faith is a lifelong evolution and no matter how long we live, it can continue to grow to the point where we have ultimate trust in God."

"With enough consideration, I would expect that there is some deeper understanding to all apparent contradictions in the Bible. It may not be easy to come by, but I'd bet when just the right circumstances of our lives develop, an understanding of these contradictions allows us to understand our own contradictions," Cowboy observed.

"What about you?" Jason asked. "Any blatant contradictions you're willing to share?"

"Oh, my old age has made me more of a big picture kind of guy. I try to catch hold of the large sweeping questions first before I get too far into the details."

"Any big examples?" Jason insisted.

"Well, the most obvious is based in the depth of monotheism. Let me establish a base of beliefs to build upon and maybe you can recognize the contradictions. Do you believe in God?" Cowboy asked.

"Oh, you mean me? Of course, I do."

"I had to ask," Cowboy explained. "We're building a base of belief here, and that is the foundation upon which we must begin this construction. You believe in God. Good. Do you believe that He is a God of love; that He is the creator of all things in the universe; and that He knows everything...every hair on your head?" Cowboy offered the questions up quicker so as not to frustrate Jason with the apparent simplicity of the conversation.

"Yes," Jason answered. "God of love, all-knowing and creator of all things."

"How about this. Do you believe that God is a God of intent? What I mean is do you believe that God knows exactly what He is doing, has a plan, and is intentional with all that He does?"

"Yes," Jason said. "Absolutely."

"Now that we have that foundation of belief confirmed, we recognize that it is pretty much the same foundation of belief that every Christian has, don't you think?" Cowboy was searching the young man's eyes for confirmation.

"Yes. That's exactly what I would say." Jason did begin to show a slight wear of frustration with the exercise of simplicity.

"Well then," Cowboy's eyes narrowed as he turned in his seat to look at Jason directly, "wouldn't we have to conclude that God created Satan? Wouldn't He have had to do it intentionally, out of love for us, and for a purpose?"

Jason took a moment to digest the implications brought into the discussion. He could not immediately agree with the concept of premeditated evil, but he also couldn't find any hole in the logic.

"Let me throw another wrench into the gears that are whirring in your head right now," Cowboy offered without giving this young conversationalist much time to recover. "Christ teaches us to love our enemies. It would, of course, follow that we identify the enemy and ask who, exactly, is this enemy? If we are righteous men and are confronted with struggles of many kinds offered by our enemies, wouldn't these enemies be driven by sin, and hence, by Satan?"

For the first time since their conversation began, Jason found himself without words. "Lucifer," he finally offered, "Lucifer was God's most beloved angel when he rebelled, taking half of the angels of heaven with him in revolt. He was jealous of God, wanting to be God, and he became the fallen angel."

"Oh, I understand," Cowboy nodded, "but God had to know it was going to happen. It is exactly why He created Lucifer; to either rebel against Him or follow His instructions by being fully faithful to Him. I guess the real question is why? What was the purpose of doing so?"

Both men sat quietly while Jason mentally chewed over his thoughts. The landing gear splashing into the outside air turbulence and the flight attendant's announcements were lost to the sudden death of the discussion. "Remember, George Bernard Shaw once said that all great truths begin as blasphemies. Could there be a more blasphemous idea within the Biblical truth?"

Jason was visualizing the contradiction while his eyes danced back and forth across the field of vision. With a look of concern, Cowboy exhausted his supply of queries and Jason couldn't find a word anywhere near his voice. The bouncing of the jet against the runway shook the young traveler out of his vacant gawk and Cowboy offered a soothing thought.

"It's all right," he explained. "You are a brilliant young man; far brighter than I ever was at your age. This career you've chosen is filled with brilliant people and I do not fancy myself as one of them.

These brilliant people will be looking to you for understanding, and they demand that you make sense with your guidance. That insistence is what makes them brilliant."

As the plane stopped and the jetway rolled to the door, Cowboy reiterated, "Remember, there are reasons for these apparent contradictions. Here's my contact information," he said, offering him a business card. "I cannot remember the last time I enjoyed a conversation so much, and if you'd like, you are most welcome to contact me any time to continue it." Cowboy's concern was replaced with a genuine smile.

As they strode down the jetway with Jason to his left, Cowboy noticed the right corner of Jason's mouth curl slightly upward in a mischievous half smile. "Father Billings might have a handful when classes start again Monday."

"Father Billings?" Cowboy halted mid-stride. "Father Charles Billings?" It was Cowboy's turn to look stunned while the deplaning passengers stacked behind them irritated. With a light bump at his back, Cowboy and Jason increased their pace up the jetway.

"Yeah," Jason informed him with a puzzled expression. "Father Charles Billings. He teaches our Old Testament course."

"Last year that old sod was teaching graduate students and had three interns. What the hell is he doing teaching Old Testament to freshmen?" Cowboy and Jason were now standing in the terminal in front of the restrooms.

"No way!" Jason exclaimed. "You know Father Billings? Well, of course you know Father Billings. Why wouldn't you know Father Billings? I can't believe you know Father Billings!" Jason's enthusiasm earned a glance from several departing travelers milling around the bathrooms waiting for their companions. "He is the BEST! and the reason I came back early from our fall break."

Cowboy was uncomfortably wearing an expression of confusion. "Hold on, hold on, hold on." He had his palms facing Jason chest high. "Why would Father Billings be teaching freshmen theology?" Cowboy's expression changed to one of parental patience.

"Actually, I'm in the higher two hundred level theology classes because of my application for admission. It was kind of an honorary thing that the theology department allowed since they thought the freshmen level classes would be too boring for me." Jason paused waiting for some comment of approval, getting nothing more from Cowboy than the same quiet expression of restrained patience. "Oh...well...yes, he has been teaching undergraduate classes this year, and really only three days a week. Yay for us!"

Still nothing from Cowboy but the continuous, uncomfortable eye contact that would soon develop into a glare if his question lingered much longer. "Yeah...right," Jason continued with a slight nod. "The board of regents thought this was the best thing that Father Billings could do. He's kind of in a part-time teaching mode with underclassmen while getting his treatments."

"What do you mean *treatments*? Has he undertaken some sort of beautifying spa regimen? Have they discovered a way to cure his bald spot? What kind of treatments?" Cowboy's voice was slightly elevated; less patient and flavored with a mild panic. He already knew what treatments, but he was afraid he had to hear it announced anyway.

Jason chuckled lightly at Cowboy's questions, but that quickly faded into seriousness. "He was diagnosed with cancer at the beginning of the semester and he is going in for his fourth treatment at the University Medical Center tomorrow. That's why I came back early before classes started again next week. A bunch of us guys are getting together tomorrow afternoon to go visit him. You know, pick up his spirits."

Although he hadn't realized it, Cowboy's expression changed to one of subdued anger. "Fourth out of how many treatments?"

Jason could tell that Cowboy wanted to bark, but appreciated that he hadn't. Still, he had asked the question loud enough to gain a few glances of his own from bathroom stragglers.

"Fourth of sixteen," Jason responded with his own look of concern now. "Do you two know each other well?"

"No," Cowboy forced the answer out, then softened a little. "No. We had done some work together last year is all." He thought, *That's how I know that old prick of misery.*

Jason walked him to the Lota Coffee stand that Cowboy found blessedly open. The thoughts firing through Cowboy's mind on the way explained everything. Sixteen treatments meant it was serious. Cutting him back to part-time undergraduate teaching meant it was serious. Giving him a subject as unchallenging as Old Testament theology meant it was serious. *He probably had to fight to get the board of regents to allow that,* Cowboy thought.

Jason had a sheepish look, like he had said something wrong and couldn't take it back, so he remained quiet, leaving Cowboy to his thoughts. Cowboy ordered a large dark roast coffee and requested an extra shot of espresso. Then he turned and smiled widely at his young friend and took his hand, pumping it twice firmly. "I cannot tell you how much I've enjoyed our conversation and meeting you, sir. You truly are a remarkable young man; far more impressive than your counterparts twice your age."

Jason smiled back and firmed his grip. "Thank you," he stated, and shook Cowboy's hand right back. "If it's not too much to ask, would you mind if I emailed you...maybe keep the discussion going a while?"

"I hope you will." Cowboy laughed. "You send me an email first chance you get so that I have your contact information. I promise I'll get back to you right away."

"Excellent! I've got some classmates waiting to pick me up downstairs, so gotta run, but you travel safe. It was great meeting you."

"You too, Jace." Cowboy smiled back. "I'm really looking forward to connecting again. I'll let you know when I'm in the neighborhood and we can have lunch." He no more than finished the word lunch when the young man turned and began sprinting toward the escalator.

4

THE ANGRY PRIEST

I.

C owboy knew the drive home would be a long one. It was past midnight after a long day's work and he didn't get the rest he had hoped for on the flight home. Between the coffee and the dull ache left by his morning tumbling routine, he should have no problem remaining alert during the drive, but he opened the window slightly as an added defense against drowsiness. He paid his parking fees and wound his way through the side streets toward the interstate. Large oak, maple, and walnut trees lined the streets and their falling leaves seasoned the air, leaving it crisp and delicious. His memories stretched for the childhood that stirred just out of reach of the contentment found in the swirling smell of autumn, but the reason for such peace that filled him in the fall remained hidden.

Glimpses of his mother's flowing hair, shining in the garden under the early morning harvest sun, danced just out of reach and his thoughts were continuing to land and dwell on Father Billings. The raspy voice of the padre barked in Cowboy's memory, reminding him that the priest didn't care for his input, ending their visit with the father nearly bellowing. Cowboy could almost feel the priest's voice grating against his eardrum. No doubt the residual effects of being mentioned during his earlier conversation with the young seminarian.

Cowboy felt the voice tingling in his tail bone, creeping up his spine. His encounter with the priest the year before while he conducted his inspections on Creighton's campus left them both with an emotional toothache. When the tingling rose to the back of his neck, "He's sick," was all it had to say.

I know! Cowboy's thought fired back. *Jason already told me that he's sick.* Cowboy's mind was racing ahead of his emotions, opening his availability for first thing in the morning. *I could go down and take care of several inspections coming due near campus. If I take off before daylight, I could be done early enough to visit him at the University Medical Center before lunch. That would give us a chance to visit before Jason and his classmates show up tomorrow afternoon to lift his spirits.*

Slow down there, Cowboy argued with himself. *I don't want to get up before dawn and I don't want to go visit that old crab.*

His truck shot up the on-ramp to the interstate, filling the cab with autumn's spiced air. The tip of his left ear grew icy, forcing him to roll up the window.

You slow down, Hothead, his mind retorted. *Literally...slow down or get a ticket. You always drive like a maniac when you're mad. This isn't about what you want, dumb ass. This is about what he needs.*

In the middle of this warming debate within himself, Cowboy set his cruise control to three miles an hour over the limit, took a sip of his coffee, and emotionally retreated from the battle. He knew he was right. He could free up the morning to do inspections near campus and by lunch he could stop over to visit Father Billings; maybe even buy him a meal at a neighboring restaurant. *There... you see? I knew you'd figure it out*, his mind thought with a victorious little half smile.

"Piss off, smart ass," Cowboy responded out loud to add finality to the debate. His mind bolted after the memories of the previous year's visit with Father Billings. He had been doing the certificate inspections of the last half of the boilers and pressure vessels on Creighton's campus, and Father Billings had taken on the role of escorting Cowboy to the fourteen objects requiring his attention. While their casual conversation began blithely enough, it did not end quite so casually.

II.

"Good morning," Cowboy said to the Engineering Department secretary, staring glassy-eyed at her computer screen, as he approached her counter. She started a bit and snapped her head up to see the thin figure approaching on long strides while lifting the Stetson off his head. "I have an appointment to conduct the boiler inspections today," and while looking down at his clipboard, Cowboy added, "The contact name given here is J. Bronson."

"Oh," she responded. "That's right. I remember seeing this on Jerry's calendar, but he's not in at the moment." Cowboy looked just past the young secretary at the wall of windows and the door behind her desk. The door was labeled *Eng. Dept. Manager*, under which was stenciled *J. Bronson*. The desk inside the office was in disarray and the chair was pushed back. The southern side of the office was a wall of books behind the desk, and in front of it was a round conference table equipped with four wooden chairs, a technical manual opened to a centerfold drawing, and two Creighton University coffee mugs. The far wall in the office was also made of large glass panels, with only one of several louvered shades left hanging about a foot from its bottom. The other three large shades were pulled completely up and the bright winter sun filled the room. Cowboy could see the pedestrian traffic scurrying across the center of the snow-covered campus. Leafless trees and undisturbed park benches were perfectly aligned and blanketed with snow.

"Emergencies happen without warning," Cowboy told the young lady. "That's what makes them emergencies." He smiled as he looked down at Miranda Reagan, learning her name from the wedding and graduation announcement left opened on her desk. Miss Reagan furrowed her brow slightly. She was early twenty-something and cute as a bug's ear with the crease between her thick eyebrows caused by her furrowing from wondering how this tall, thin stranger knew of Jerry's family emergency. "Lucky fellow." Cowboy smiled, spotting the modest engagement ring on her left hand.

She rolled her engagement ring between her thumb and index finger with a smile. "It was an early Christmas present from my high school sweetheart. We've set the date for the last week in May." Cowboy could tell that the young lady was very excited about her pending nuptials.

"You tell young David that he is a lucky fellow indeed, and smart too, having waited until you finished college before walking you down the aisle." Miss Reagan's brow creased again when her smile faded and she returned to her furrowing. Before she could ask, Cowboy said, "So who would I talk to about these inspections that I've come to do?"

"Ah," Miranda started a bit again with a slight bounce in her seat. "Let me call Father Billings to see what he'd like us to do." She picked up the phone and punched three numbers. Cowboy could hear the faint purring of the ringer and the raspy answer of Father Billings. At that distance from the receiver and on the phone, his voice sounded almost like an animal growling. Miranda explained the situation and thanked him as she hung up. "Father Billings will be right with you." She paused and furrowed again at Cowboy. "Do you mind if I ask how you knew my fiancé's name?"

"Not at all. You have a wedding and a graduation announcement on your desk. Although the graduation announcement is covering the last names written on the wedding announcement, your full name does appear on the graduation invitation. Your engagement ring is new and the semester usually ends the middle of May. Although I cannot read your signature, I can see you've been practicing signing it on your note pad lying near your mouse. Being here usually means you would have to sign for a lot of packages for parts, tools, and the like. No doubt you want to practice signing with your new name." Cowboy smiled down at the young lady. After a brief pause he added, "It's really just a matter of practice."

She collected the announcements and tossed them into the top drawer of her desk as Father Billings opened the door.

"Good morning." Cowboy held out his hand.

"Ah. Hang on there." Father Billings showed Cowboy his palm and turned to the secretary. "Tell me again, Miranda. What's this all about?"

"Well," Cowboy started.

Father Billings interrupted by raising his exposed palm to Cowboy a little higher. He then pointed his index finger at the secretary and said, "I'm asking her."

"Well," Miranda started, "this gentleman had an appointment with Mr. Bronson to do broiler inspections today, but Mr. Bronson got called out on a family emergency earlier, so I called you to see if there was someone else who could be his escort."

Father Billings crumpled his face behind his thick glasses and gave Miranda a puzzled look. That spurred Cowboy into another rescue attempt. "I believe she means *boiler*, not *broiler*. The certificates from the state are expiring next month, so renewal inspections were scheduled for today."

"And what is it that you need?"

"Really just an escort around campus to open the doors and someone I can make recommendations to, in case there are any," Cowboy answered.

"Oh," Miranda bounced from her seat. "I know." She padded across the floor into Bronson's office. Both men watched as she danced around his desk and reached up to the exposed side of the library panel and plucked off a large ring of keys, bringing them back to her desk by the same route. She laid the assembly into Father Billings' cupped hands. The ring holes of each key sported a color-coded tab that she lightly tugged at while explaining. "The white ones are places for storage. The blue ones are for tool boxes, and the red ones are for machinery spaces. I just organized all of these for Jerry...uh, Mr. Bronson...just last week by tying these tags to them."

"And how am I supposed to know where each one goes?" Father Billings scowled down at the tangle in his cupped hands.

"Oh. Look here." Miranda cocked her head to the right while sliding a red tag between her thumb and index finger. "I typed the location where each key goes right here on the tag. See here? Where it says Student Union Basement? That means when you go over to the student union, go down into the basement and find the door with the red label on it. It will say boiler room or machinery space." She enunciated *boiler* to let Father Billings know she had it down now. "This key opens that door," Miranda finished with a wide smile.

Father Billings was squinting hard through his thick glasses and holding the pile of keys very close to his nose by then. "Well," he said, looking up at Cowboy. "Will that work for you?"

"Why, that's brilliant," Cowboy offered with a nodding smile at Miranda. "Well done." Miranda smiled back and blushed slightly for the compliment received in front of the professor.

"Then let's get this show on the road," Father Billings ordered in his raspy voice.

III.

"How long is this going to take you?" Father Billings queried.

"Mr. Bronson staggered the renewal dates for each half of the objects that require inspections by six months. He also organized it so that there are two zones, one for each expiration date, so we'll only have to do half of them in the same general location today. That will make it easy," Cowboy explained, then added, "Your Mr. Bronson is a pretty sharp nut," with a smile.

Father Billings just squinted deeper through his heavy glasses at Cowboy while carrying the keys in his cupped hands in front of his chest.

"Um..." Cowboy said, "we should be done by lunchtime." Father Billings nodded, handing Cowboy the mess of keys with his right hand while sweeping his left arm out in front of them in an *after you* fashion, indicating to Cowboy that he should stop talking and proceed, which he was more than happy to do.

Of the fourteen inspections that were scheduled, five of them were completed before either man spoke again. Armed with a campus map and in possession of the keys to the kingdom, Cowboy really didn't need Father Billings to accompany him, but university rules mandated that visitors have escorts. "How long were you in the Navy?" Father Billings croaked from behind Cowboy in the middle of his sixth inspection in the kitchen area of the staff lounge. The unexpected question startled him a bit, but Cowboy did not look up from his clipboard while noting the conditions found on the water heater relief valve.

"Six years, but I've been out for a long time," Cowboy answered as he turned to face the priest with an intrigued expression.

"Not long enough. Your boots are wearing a fine layer of polish, shirt is neatly pressed and it, and your tee shirt, are tightly tucked into your waistband." Father Billings raised and lowered his index finger while pointing at his chest and belly button. "Your gig line is straight as a string, and your hair is short. You carry two pens, one for backup and both in black ink. The military never allowed blue ink. You print in capital letters, you do not lollygag, but carry about your work with intent. I might have guessed Marines by your build and the way you still walk, with your feet a little too far apart as if you are trying to balance on a moving object...like a ship, but the facial hair and the fact that you seem to know equipment suggests Navy instead. A marine wouldn't know a boiler from a broiler." Father Billings would have had a smirk of satisfaction on his face, except he knew he was correct and no smirk was necessary. He thought about smiling at the reference to Ms. Reagan's earlier description of broiler inspections, but then decided against it.

The priest noted that Cowboy lacked amazement, but he was impressed, if only mildly. As he sat against the front edge of the parts bench facing Cowboy, he held his hands palms up on either side of his waist. "What about you? What do you think?"

Cowboy did not avert his eyes from the priest when he used his pen to reach behind his right shoulder and point directly at the relief valve's discharge port. "The sediment collecting at the relief valve discharge tells me that this thing is probably leaking in service and needs to be replaced."

"Not what I meant."

Cowboy's shoulders sagged slightly and his head lowered. "I know." He scrutinized the priest with a weary expression. "You weren't always a priest. A military man yourself based upon the impeccable neatness of your clothing and your matter-of-factness. The age spots showing heavily on your neck, forehead, bridge of your nose, and back of your hands, I would say you have definitely spent a considerable amount of your youth under a tropical sun. Those callouses on your hands are permanent and there is no question you have done your time digging, chopping, packing, and pulling. Clearing landing zones, digging foxholes, pulling supply ropes, and carrying rifles, and the amount of white hair would have me guessing a Vietnam combat veteran. The way it is still cut would say Marines."

"Anything else?" Father Billings asked the expressionless inspector after removing his glasses and cleaning the lenses with a kerchief pulled from his right front pant pocket.

Cowboy sighed. He wanted to like this man, but it was like wanting to hug a porcupine. There is no good approach to even start. "I can't begin to say what circumstances might have arisen to lead you here, but it was a heavy price. The missing right earlobe and the direction of taper of that straight scar leading from it down to nearly the corner of your mouth, and the missing tip of your right pinky finger could be fading remnants of that cost. You appear old enough to retire, but still not old enough to account for the rate of deterioration of your vision, and you certainly didn't get into the Marines with vision that bad."

Without Billings' heavy glasses, Cowboy could almost see the young man underneath the layers of age and scars. While Father Billings certainly was not the man he used to be, he would still be tougher than boot leather for any man twenty years his junior. "I suspect the fading vision might have resulted from the dry eyes caused by the use of opiates; perhaps those found in morphine that is injected into a wounded soldier during battlefield triage. The amount of morphine necessary to cause this condition would have had to be excessive, meaning these were grievous injuries that were probably incurred more than once."

"Is that it?" the priest asked, noticing the saddened demeanor growing in his guest.

"Isn't that enough?"

The priest set his heavy glasses back on his nose and squinted at the face of his wristwatch. "I expect so," he said softly. "We'd better stop this jacking around and get the job done."

With Father Billings in tow, Cowboy led to the next three buildings where inspections were due before either man spoke again. "So, are you a churchgoing man? Do you believe in God?" The effort to overcome the hesitation of the priest to ask the questions made them sound as if two were stuffed in a package only capable of holding one.

Cowboy stopped his walk to the tenth building and turned to face the priest following him. He couldn't pass up an opportunity to learn everything he could from this man, whether it pissed the priest off or not. "Make a deal with you, Padre," Cowboy offered.

Father Billings winced at the title *padre*, not because he had any arrogance or sense of propriety, but because this smart-ass used the term as a mockery of his profession. Still, he was intrigued. The term smart-ass didn't accurately summarize this fellow, although that was close. "Less of a smart-ass and more of a wild man." He mumbled, "That's precisely what I think he might be." "What kind of a deal? And don't call me Padre," the priest ordered.

Cowboy looked the priest dead in the eye and made an executive decision: never, EVER call him Padre again. "Sorry. I meant no disrespect." It was true. Cowboy was actually just trying to alleviate the intensity of this man. As he turned back to walk toward the next building, he offered, "How about we get a little quid pro quo going here? I expect you're not really interested in social pleasantries and our time is limited to only four more of these inspections. What do you say? You game?"

"All right. Since I've already started, do you believe in God?" he asked again.

Cowboy knew the priest wasn't really interested in whether he believed in God or not, but the *why* or *why not* of his answer was what really stabbed the spade of interest into the digging. The first question was usually designed to identify the X mark of where the digging for treasure was to begin.

"Yes." Cowboy answered him matter-of-factly.

"And how did you come by this belief?"

"Whoa now. I believe I've answered your question truthfully," Cowboy announced. "I think it's my turn at bat."

"Fair enough."

"Do you believe the Catholic Church fully supports, emulates, and administers the teachings of Jesus Christ?"

"I believe it does the best it knows how to do exactly that," Father Billings answered with an almost imperceptible hesitation... almost. The priest's hesitation was in recognizing the 'X' where this wild man intended to start digging. The two arrived at the next location and Cowboy immediately commenced his inspection duties. "Why do you believe in God?" The priest threw out his next question like it was too hot for his mind to handle.

"Through my considerations, I find that man must be, at his very core, good, and that means that God must exist. The only other alternative is that there is no good or evil, and if that were the case, man could not exist in this manner," Cowboy explained, holding his right hand up and waving it in front of them to bring attention to their surroundings. "Because the concept of good and evil exists, God must exist, and man must be elementally good."

"I have seen what a man can do to another man and might argue that, at his very core, he is evil," Father Billings suggested through a haunting stare.

"As have I, and that is an argument that can only have a losing outcome. The fact that we recognize it as evil only substantiates that we are elementally good," Cowboy finished. "How does the act of excommunication support the teachings of Jesus Christ?" Cowboy took his turn.

Father Billings began rubbing his clean-shaven chin while

Cowboy finished his inspections. He was still rubbing his chin when they departed for the next building. When they unlocked the basement door and Cowboy began his task, the priest finally spoke. "Most of us feel that the Bible is a book about God written by all of these people. I believe a more accurate description might be that it is a book written by God about all of these people. If the Bible were about God and written by all of these people, it would be an imperfect book about a perfect being, but were it written by God about all of these people, it would be a perfect book, written about all of these imperfect beings." The priest did not smile or even nod with satisfaction. He simply stared at the back of his lenses and asked, "If man is good, why does he destroy everything?"

Now it was Cowboy's turn to be quiet. He puzzled through the next two inspections, trying to understand the implications of what the priest had just told him until the weighty thought finally landed on him point first. If the Bible were written by people, it could not achieve the perfection necessary to encapsulate an understanding of a perfect being, leaving it flawed by the authors. But if the Bible were written by a perfect being, the interpretations made by these imperfect beings would, to them, leave it endlessly flawed.

Catholicism would then be a simple imperfect interpretation of a perfect book written by a perfect being. If that is true, then everything is an imperfect interpretation. That would leave the act of excommunication by the church explained as a simple misinterpretation. *Of course*, Cowboy thought in amazement. *Everything is wrong, then, to some degree...everything. It is possible to postulate now that all of the world's pain is generated within this degree of imperfection. Every act of genocide, every act of war, every starving person, every act of human trafficking, all the way down to every abused child and every failed marriage is the result of people measuring and comparing their degree of imperfection.*

"Man destroys everything because he is furious with his imperfection," Cowboy finally answered.

"Hmmm," Father Billings responded, but with his raspy voice, it sounded more like growling and less like pondering. The two men finished the remaining inspections in silence. Cowboy was certain he had offended the priest through his queries of the Catholic faith, noting his already prickly demeanor sharpened as they returned to the office where Miranda was organizing the bottom drawer of the filing cabinet behind her counter.

Miranda looked up when she heard the door open and felt the whoosh of cold air. Father Billings poked his thumb over his right shoulder at Cowboy when his eyes met the secretary's. "Make sure you get whatever notes he's made and get them to Jerry when he gets back tomorrow." Cowboy stopped at Miranda's counter, but the priest kept walking without saying good-bye or even offering a parting glance. He did manage a "thank you, Miranda" before the door to the main lobby of the building closed behind him.

"That was abrupt," Cowboy offered the young secretary while watching the priest exit.

"Oh, Father Billings is a busy man and I'm sure he has other appointments." Miranda took the inspection notes Cowboy had made while they continued looking toward the door the priest had just exited. The bright noon sun bounced off a shiny object quickly passing across the cold campus outside of Jerry's office and flashed across the inspector's eyes, causing him to squint.

5

THOSE IN NEED

I.

Headlights flashed across Cowboy's field of vision, causing him to squint at the sleepy main street in front of him. His eyes opened in astonishment when he recognized that he was only two blocks from his house, but had no recollection of the last seventy-five minutes of driving. He lifted the Lotta Coffee cup out of its holder in the truck console and found it lukewarm and full.

He remembered taking a sip, paying for his parking, and shooting up the on ramp of the interstate engaging himself in an argument. He started thinking about taking off at sunrise to visit Father Billings and then blinking furiously at the high beams that painfully flared into his pupils within two blocks of his driveway. Of the interceding seventy-six miles, he had been completely unable to recollect a single one.

That's a little eerie, he thought. *I've got to start working fewer hours in a day and traveling less at night. Going to end up in the ditch wearing that steering wheel as a necklace.* He shut his headlights off and banged the screen door open, propping it against his hip while unlocking the front door. He was tired and only wanted two more aspirin and a soft bed.

He noticed the swelling on the back of his head had subsided and the ache behind his eyes dulled, but two more tablets would likely do wonders for keeping him asleep tonight. He was planning on getting back on the road right at sunrise, and four hours of sleep were going to be necessary.

As he slung his rucksack back on its hook on the side panel of his library, he bumped the mouse sitting quietly on its pad next to his desktop computer's keyboard. The movement caused the computer monitor to flash into life, and the glare of his inbox now lit the room. *Bad idea*, he thought, but before he could close his email and shut down the screen, he noticed thirty-one new emails received today. Most of them were related to work and could wait until tomorrow after lunch. There were also several people with the utmost sincerity offering ways of helping him overcome his erectile dysfunction, absolutely free vacations to the Bahamas, and two more that needed his help transferring millions of dollars of inherited money into bank accounts in the United States.

Cowboy considered helping the poor family in Africa to transfer those funds without even accepting the generous fee offered, and ordering his free sample of the medications to cure erectile dysfunction, although he could never recall suffering from the affliction. In the end, he decided he didn't have time for a vacation right now, free or not, and he threw all advertisements into the desktop trash can with a satisfying clank.

There were four emails, however, that seemed to insist on a response right now, at 1:41 on a Tuesday morning, after spending far too many hours bouncing down to Houston and back through the course of an uncommonly busy Monday. The last one received, which showed as the first one on his list, was from the young seminarian who captured his imagination on the return flight from Houston. *That can wait until morning*, Cowboy thought. *I'm just sure it can, can't it?* He wasn't fully convinced, but would continue to argue the point while he looked at the other three.

The next in line was from Mike. At first glance, it appeared that he was just returning a report after doing a peer review, but he was apologizing for being tardy with his response and explained he and his wife Sue were distraught over the loss of Izzy, one of their four dogs, and the third of the four to have passed away in recent months. Condolences should never wait. Mike was a dear friend and mentor and absolutely crazy about his dogs. There was Lady, Grace, Pepe, and Izzy, and of the four, Pepe and Izzy were his constant companions.

They were smaller lap dogs, mongrels from the same litter that were never anywhere but next to Mike when he was home. They shared food, slept in the same bed, sat and watched the news together. It did not seem imaginable that one would ever be without the other two. They were, without question, two of the best companion dogs Cowboy had ever met, and an exemplary reflection of their owner.

Izzy had fallen ill with a respiratory disorder some time previously and had managed to cough and hack her way to a fourteen-year life span before the time came. Mike's email simply stated, *"Apologies for the delay in getting this back to you, but we had to put Izzy down today. This is a very well written report and complete and I only had to make a couple of changes. I think you are not needing me anymore. We've been out of sorts here because of Izzy's passing. I still get very red faced and swear I've smelled her with me. Sounds crazy but it's true."*

Any comfort that Cowboy could offer was needed as soon as he could deliver it. Anyone who was not a dog lover might not understand, but anyone who is knows that no matter how well a dog is loved, it will likely not outlive its owner. He replied directly from his heart. *"Not needing you anymore?? What a load of hogwash! I may not live long enough to fully comprehend all you have taught me about engineering and rotating machines, for these things you have taught will take me a lifetime to contemplate. On the other hand, you may not live long enough to fully comprehend all you've taught me about honesty, integrity, fairness and joy, for these things you have taught will take me a lifetime to demonstrate. I cannot think of anything more needed than your continued input, regardless of the subject matter.*

"As for Izzy, I cannot avoid tearing up myself. Good dogs are a direct reflection of good owners. The measure of a man's depth shows in the nature of his dog, and Izzy, Lady, and Grace all reflected so well of you and your lovely bride. I have spent a good deal of study on the science and philosophy of the dog. They fascinate me with their abilities and comic relief. Ann Landers once advised, 'We should not accept our dog's admiration as conclusive evidence that we are wonderful.' She's right. I may not be wonderful, but my dog doesn't care. She loves me anyway.

"It is the very nature of a dog, the way they love you anyway, that I find so compelling. What do you suppose they dream about while lying in front of the fireplace with their feet wagging in a running half step, sounding their muffled barks? Ben Williams once said that there is no psychiatrist in the world like a puppy licking your face. I think that is also true. Everyone needs this sense of being loved, and your dog cannot wait to fulfill that need.

"Henry Ward Beecher was quoted as saying that the dog was created especially for children. 'He is the god of frolic.' Again, as for my dog, it is true. She never chooses to stay in and watch TV over going outside to romp around with me. She understands that I am just a big kid and reminds me every day that I must make time to play, especially with her.

"Certainly, Izzie is romping with Lady and Grace now. Did you know that the dog is mentioned in the Bible eighteen times? The cat...not even once. I suspect James Thurber's assessment of traditional theology was sound when he said, 'If I have any beliefs about immortality, it is that certain dogs I have known will go to heaven, and very, very few persons.'

"I have always thought that the love I have for God may one day find Him opening the pearly gates, inviting me into His house; but the love my dogs have for me will find them rushing through those gates to greet me and to welcome me home.

"Don't worry. I have every confidence that all of them are waiting for you at the front door. Just make sure they have a very long wait, as I still have considerable need for you right here."

II.

Cowboy's eyes dropped down to the next email in his inbox and noted it was from Christy. The first words of her memo were "I am so sorry," and this piqued his concern. "What's up with my little guardian angel?"

Christy's email was brief, but heavy with burden. *"I am so sorry it took so long to get back to you. Because I know you are a friend, I am going to share what is going on in my life and sidetracking me more than I'd like to admit. My oldest son is dealing with anxiety and depression. He has three boys ages 5, 3 and 1. I have been doing a lot of babysitting and worrying.*

"My youngest sister just found out that she may have breast cancer. She had a biopsy yesterday, so we should have more information on Monday. Waiting is the hardest, especially now that my mom passed away last Saturday and the funeral is coming up.

"I have shed a lot of tears so I apologize for being sidetracked. Did you find out the dates for your upcoming trip to Abu Dhabi? If you have a chance, please send those to me and I will review your travel options. So sorry and thank you!"

"Poor Christy," was all Cowboy could say. "Oh, that poor woman. She must be on the verge of an implosion with all this hitting her at once." Cowboy began rubbing his forehead directly under his hairline with his thumb and first finger. He discovered years ago that massaging this area somehow had the effect of quieting his mind and stirring his brain for the words needed at the moment, and there had been many times when he had rubbed the hide off his scalp futilely searching for the right words.

"I have not received the travel dates just yet, but hope to hear soon. Once I do, I'll let you know. More importantly is how you are dealing with the world. Family is not what sidetracks us from work, Dearest. It is work that sidetracks us from family. If I might be so bold as to impose a few thoughts on these matters, it may help. Of course, there is always the possibility that it may not, but I'm willing to risk it.

"Young men, such as your son, are imposed upon by an impossible

social definition of success in today's world. If they're not indepen-
dently wealthy, driving Porsche turbos and marrying supermodels,
it becomes too easy for them to feel inadequate. Young men have a
very tough go establishing roots in a high rev, consumable society,
and it leaves them feeling trapped between what they've been pro-
vided, and what they're aspiring to, which is a vacancy too large to
fill with any opportunities, and too small to allow room for real joy.

"Too often these young men, convinced they are failures, will
turn to anything that might ease that pain and keep them from car-
ing about the impossibility imposed upon them, and it blinds them
to the fact that, because they were created, they have already suc-
ceeded. Once they realize that being created is the pinnacle of suc-
cess, they can start to understand the depth of love it took to bring
that creation to fruition...the love of a mother, an aunt, a teacher, a
father, a friend, or even three young boys filled with adoration to-
ward their father. This depth of love is the only thing that can fill the
void that so many young men feel, and cures them of their anxiety
and depression. It, in fact, cures them of the world.

"Henry David Thoreau once said, 'The mass of men lead lives of
quiet desperation and go to the grave with the song still in them.'
I have a feeling that your young son is exhausted with the quiet
desperation. He only needs to realize that his song is not subject to
the world's approval, and only his own matters. Then he will allow
himself to sing.

"A lot of babysitting is very helpful, but worrying never is...ever.
As difficult as it is, you must let those tears fall and leave them lay.
Put that worry down and leave it be. Every time you pick it up, wor-
ry besets you and that never helps...ever.

"The fact that you are a mother insists that you are also a wom-
an of faith, whether chosen or not, because you had enough faith to
bring a child into this world. And because you are a woman of faith,
you've no need to worry. Patience will be far more helpful to your
son. Patience and guidance toward the only thing that can fill the
vacancy left by a world that will never know or care for him the way
you do; a level of patience that will last his entire life if necessary.

---

*The kind of patience that only a grandmother might have. You can-
not be patient, offer guidance, or demonstrate faith while worrying.*

*"Something tells me your little sister will be just fine. It may be
easy to perceive such a statement as cavalier, but I lost a young
niece, still in her twenties with three young sons of her own, to
breast cancer. Not a cavalier statement at all, but one made with a
confidence that can only be had by a man of faith.*

*"Whether her test comes back negative, or her catching it early
with the advancements in medical treatments at her disposal, she
will be fine whatever the case...honest. It is what she stands to learn
from the circumstances that will help her along her path. It is her
realization that, as R. W. Emerson stated, 'It is not the length of life
that matters, but the depth of life' that will bring your young sister
to a place where she will begin to live deeply.*

*"I am so very sorry to hear of the loss of your mother. It always
helps me to keep with the understanding that none of us will avoid
such inevitably. Your momma's suffering is over and now we can
recognize all of the joy her entirety was spent in leaving that joy
here with us; in her children, her grandchildren, and even her great-
grandchildren. As we still recognize her here, we learn where our
own joy originates, how it grows within us, and how it becomes the
only thing we hope to outlive us. All of our lives will be spent, angel,
but knowing that makes it a life spent well.*

*"The world is a tumultuous place, Love. It is a place that none of
us belongs, and consequently, none of us will survive. Understanding
this always brings me to my favorite verse...Psalms 46:10, 'Be still
and KNOW that I am God.' Confirmation that we do not control our
circumstances, only how we respond to them. Know that you are
in these circumstances that are beyond your control for a reason,
and that reason is to always find the love that dwells within them."*
Cowboy signed his message, "Your Friend Always."

III.

The previous weekend, Cowboy had emailed a dear friend of
his named Jack after talking with Jack's cousin. His cousin informed

him that he did not think Jack would be making it to deer camp in Missouri this year, as he had not been doing well since being diagnosed with cancer. Jack had been the one who convinced Cowboy to join him in the southern Missouri forests. Cowboy loved the people, the location, and the outdoors, and had been accompanying Jack every year of the previous five for their week-long adventure, except for last season, when Jack couldn't make the trip.

It was after his conversation with Jack's cousin that Cowboy issued an email inquiring about his well-being and whether Jack thought he'd make the trip from Virginia for the upcoming hunting season. Jack replied, *"I had my second follow-up visit at the Massey Cancer Center and the cancer in my body is still smoldering around 10% involvement in my blood and bone marrow. I have had a full body x-ray and a PET scan that looks for cancer cells. At this time, I have no tumor in the bone, which is a good thing, and I'm considered to be in stage one.*

"What does that mean for Jack? As long as the cancer is smoldering I am in a two-month follow-up mode. Every two months I go for lab work to determine how much the cancer is advancing. The doctor said this could go on for two months or a year, but the cancer will advance because it is consuming my good blood cells.

"Once the involvement in my blood hits 30%, I will start treatment of 21 days of chemotherapy followed with seven days off. There will be four to six cycles, so up to six months of chemo with weekly blood tests will be necessary. Bottom line is that I can only manage short trips during this treatment time; with the major side effects of chemo is a feeling of being tired.

"Once the cancer is put into remission, I will go into the hospital for about six weeks to undergo a stem cell bone marrow transplant. My immune system will, of course, be compromised the entire time and travel will be an issue. The doctor tells me that I can travel to major cities, where medical facilities are good, but bugging out to the woods is not going to be allowed. The PET scan revealed that I had a bum left hip and shoulder from degenerative arthritis, but that's just me getting old.

"Eye surgery last week went well, but things have been out of focus since September of last year. After the second surgery, things started clearing up, but Doc said it might take a few more to get the swelling down in my retinas and to quit seeing spots.

"As soon as I lose all my hair from the radiation, I'll have to wear a bandana over my head and my one-legged, eye-patched, pirate costume will finally be complete. All that's left is a boat and a parrot willing to set sail with me. Could use a little work on my pirate yell, AAARRRRRGGGGGHHH!!

"I've gone through the woe is me, sad, frustrated, ticked-off stages of emotions and finally am in the fighting mode to beat this thing. I've concluded that getting old is not for the faint of heart and it takes some fortitude to push past 50. Life is GOOD! Thanks for asking." And he signed it, *"Friends...Jack."*

Cowboy and Jack had crossed professional paths for nearly twenty years, but working closely together over the previous eight had made them friends. Jack was one of the best men Cowboy had ever known; a good man, good husband and father, and most importantly to Jack, a good Christian. Cowboy responded in the only way he knew how; genuinely from his heart. If he responded any other way, Jack would know it instantly.

"You will remain in our prayers," he began. *"All I know, Jack, is that there is a definite decision here that only you can make regarding the intrusion of what I can most accurately describe as a son-of-a-bitch. Fighting this intruder sounds to be no less horrific than the intruder itself and I cannot know the answer. I've watched people fight these things relentlessly until they have reached the end of themselves. The degree, intensity, and outcome is unquestionably out of their hands.*

"You and I have traveled some very similar paths throughout our lives, but in this, I can only remind you of the things you already know. You are treasured. You are so deeply loved. You are a good man; not only because of your behaviors, what you've overcome, what you've surrendered, and what you hold dear, but because you are forgiven of all indiscretions. Remembering this, knowing this

deeply, will serve you well in the choice you are confronted with right now. You see, if you choose to fight this thing, then you will have the courage to fight until you have found the end of yourself, at which point, because you know this, you also know that the point in any struggle where your strength fails is just the beginning of true power.

"If you choose not to endure these horrific treatments you face, knowing these things will keep you well in your commitment to your faith. It is knowing that the brilliant influence you've had on me, and others like me, you are already healed and prepared to go home whenever called; whenever and whichever the case may be.

"Even for a good man like yourself, it may be a tremendous effort to find the upside to the circumstances, but because you know that the testing of your faith develops perseverance, you also know that deep faith brings the light of understanding into the darkest places.

"As promised, we will keep you rigorously in our prayers. I cannot offer any valid advice regarding the decisions you're facing, since I honestly could not tell you what I would do, and as unorthodox as it might seem, I'd like to ask you a favor. Remind yourself, under every breath you take from this moment on, that you are treasured by perfection, admired by others, forgiven for all, and so deeply loved by choice. Do that, and whatever the outcome; whatever you choose, will be exactly right."

IV.

Cowboy had looked again at the email he received from Jason, the young seminarian he had talked with on his return flight from Houston. *"Did you ever come to understand the apparent contradiction of why a God of love, one who is intentional, and one that knows and created everything, would have created Lucifer?"* it asked.

I'm on a roll and might as well keep going, Cowboy thought. *If this comes up in conversation while this young fellow is visiting Father Billings tomorrow, it would be nice if he could offer some* rebuttal to the likely barrage of accusations sure to follow. Cowboy set to rubbing his hairline again with added vigor to develop the best way of wording his thoughts.

"Why did God, the creator of all things, create Satan?" he started. "Excellent question, don't you think? I've heard it explained that Satan fell because he was jealous of God. Maybe...maybe not; and it would be irrelevant to the discussion if you believe that God knows everything, since He would have created Lucifer already knowing that Lucifer would fall. He couldn't be all-knowing and have that, or anything else, catch Him by surprise.

"Best place to start is at the beginning, in Eden, where Adam and Eve were tempted to eat of the forbidden fruit from the tree of knowledge. God told them they could have anything they wanted, except that they should not partake of this forbidden fruit. Of course, an all-knowing God must be exactly that, and He knew precisely what they would do long before He told them not to do it.

"It's easy enough to know that; more difficult to understand it. I used to say that as a young man, I knew so much more than I understood, so how about we let an old man take things a little deeper. Let's look at the aspect of unconditional love that is in God's nature. He loves us endlessly, truly, and unconditionally, and I believe He wants us to understand exactly what that means. See, Adam and Eve loved God, but they really had no choice in the act. They had no idea how to do anything else...that is until they ate from the tree of knowledge of good and evil.

"If God had told them not to eat the apple, they would have had no choice but to obey, since they knew no other thing to do. God had to introduce the act of temptation by providing a tempter; hence the serpent arrives and provides us with the choice to do something other than the only thing we know to do, with God of course, fully aware that we would do it long before it happened. It was exactly why this tempter was created; to provide us with a choice between God and anything else.

"Why would this all-knowing God of love create a path of temptation for His children? To give them the free will necessary to teach them the depth of His love, so that they may come to know and understand what it means to love unconditionally, as He does. This brings up the dilemma of free will under an all-knowing God.

"How can God 'know me before I was even conceived in the womb,' and free will exist? Every choice I will ever make is already known under an all-knowing God, no matter how hard I fight the notion. Is He all-knowing, or not? The answer lies in His unconditional love for us. The single most important quality of God's love is that, in order for it to be unconditional, it must be chosen. The love we had for God in Eden before we could differentiate between good and evil was not unconditional, since we had no choice in the matter. He gave us a choice; to eat the fruit or not. He provided a tempter, since a God of love could not tempt us Himself, knowing perfectly well what we would do, and He did it to teach us the unconditional quality of His love.

"Yes, we have the free will of choice, but we all get to make the same, single choice, to choose love unconditionally and experience the joy of that, or anything else. We cannot control our circumstances under an all-knowing God; only our response to the circumstances that He has seen fit to put us in, as Paul demonstrated in his joy even while being incarcerated for thirteen long years. We can choose to be joyful, no matter what circumstances God has us in.

"He provided us the perfect example of this unconditional love, and showed us how to choose it regardless of our circumstances. A son of a carpenter in no particular position of prestige; a king born in a cave near Bethlehem; a man nearly beaten to death and hung on a cross to die after doing no wrong; and still Jesus chose love. He chose it regardless of His circumstances to show us that we can do the same.

"He explained it to us in 1 Corinthians. He defined it for us in extravagant detail, showing that we have nothing of value, can do nothing of value, and can say nothing of any value without love. Of the three that remained; faith, hope, and love, the greatest of these is love, because it must be chosen every second of every day. It is that single choice that is given us; the entirety of our free will; that *makes love the most powerful thing in the universe. There is no war that can be waged against love and won.*

"*God so loved us that He gave us this choice in Eden by sacrificing the precious innocence of His children. He demonstrated that we must choose it regardless of our circumstances by sacrificing His only son. He wants us to understand the love He has for us, by being willing to sacrifice ourselves for each other; 'A greater love has not a man than the one who gives his life for his friends.' I think we should qualify that and say, a greater love might be the man who gives his life for his enemies.*

"*Isn't that where the true sacrifice is that Christ teaches? Love your enemies, even if it kills you. Who is the enemy? What is his purpose? How is he defeated? All questions you will want to be very careful with as you travel the path laid before you.*"

Cowboy closed, "*Looking forward to hearing your thoughts on the subject,*" and squinted at his watch. "Ridiculous!" he barked at the weariness that suddenly fell upon him. "Two-thirty-seven and I'll need a six a.m. wake-up. Beautiful." He punched the send button before shutting down.

He stood and pushed his chair under the desk, and as his computer flashed its last burst of fluorescence, he noted its light had bounced off something in the far corner of the room. "I'll be damned," he swore, bending down to pick up the silver tin of Copenhagen that rolled out of his pocket when his chair tipped on him nearly twenty hours earlier. He had not had any of it since then, and never even noticed it missing through this unbelievably long day. He hadn't been that long without a chew since junior high school, which was far longer than Cowboy cared to remember. "I'll be damned," he said out loud. "I didn't even know to miss it. Guess I must be done with this foolishness," and he chucked the nearly full can into the bin next to his desk.

The Copenhagen did remind him to rub the diminishing knot on the back of his head as he peeled his shirt off in the bathroom mirror. He brushed his teeth and finished skinning his clothes before diving into bed and curling up into what he liked to refer to as the "fecal position" since it was pretty much how he felt, and certain of how he looked.

He lay there staring at the back of his eyelids with his thoughts drifting to the task at hand when the sun rose. The psychedelic phosphene danced and played in his vision while his mind turned to Father Billings. He had no idea what to expect when he visited him the next day and wondered if he was still pissed off. "Guess I'll find out soon enough."

His thoughts were beginning to meld together when suddenly those colorful little light flashes that everyone sees against their closed eyes conjugated at the very center of his field of vision, or field of darkness, Cowboy wasn't sure which. He could feel his mind collect all the way from his toes, building up immediately in front of this growing point of light when, like being shot down the darkened rifle barrel into an explosion of light, his consciousness blasted toward this phosphene point.

6

HOME IMPROVEMENTS

The soundless whoosh of light that surrounded me brought the familiar marble corridor and the sensation of the principal's office once again. From this domed room, I looked down the hall to the familiar doors that led to His den-library-laboratory. *I should think of something to call that room, perhaps a denlibratory.*

For the first time since coming to this place, or more accurately, being summoned to this place, it occurred to me that there must be more to it than this single hallway leading to this single room. If this were all there was, it certainly was enough, but I couldn't avoid the thought that this wasn't even close to all there was here.

I was wearing the same surgical scrub pants, but the pockets were all empty. Shirtless, I padded down the beautifully inlayed columns and colorful motifs covering the arched ceiling and lightly pushed the heavy panel door open.

"Well, there you are." God looked delighted to see me. "You look fit. Come sit on the table and we can take a closer look at you," He said with a broad, toothy smile. I looked down at myself to see if I really did look fit. I was not sure we were in agreement on that point. "Nonsense," He added. "You're healthy as a farm mule. Come. Sit."

When I looked up again, God was no longer behind that beautifully carved rolltop desk. He was squatting on a rolling stool and patting the pad of a medical examination table, complete with the little rubber-topped footstool at the end. He was wearing a magnificently white lab coat, with a stethoscope dangling off His neck, and wearing one of those ridiculous round reflective surfaces banded to His forehead. Smiling patiently, He said, "Time for your check-up."

"Well, this is new," I told Him. "Since when do I need a check-up?" I strolled to the table and stepped up on the rubber-topped footstool, spun, and flopped down on the pad.

"Your body is a temple. It is the house within which I dwell. Want to make sure you're taking care of the place." He laughed, which always causes me to laugh with Him. He started by running the handle end of His reflex hammer lengthways across the soles of my feet. I crossed my legs girly fashion as ordered and He took the business end of the same hammer and thumped the tendon under my kneecap.

He then checked my sitting position and spine alignment by running His thumbs up either side of my back. It wasn't until He got up to my shoulder blades when the first note was scribbled in His manila file. "That's quite a knot you've got there between your neck and shoulder on your left side. I notice you're also building up a nice arthritic ache in your left hip."

"Old football injury coming back to haunt me," I explained.

"I know every injury you've ever suffered, and this has nothing to do with football, or war wounds, or catastrophic childhood inventions. Those were all wounds I used to teach you," He explained. "This is something you need to teach yourself; one of your own doing. Jacob tried the same thing on Me back when I was just starting this whole thing," He laughed a loud "HA!" "Now there's an entire country named after him."

"But You're the one who crippled him." I laughed my own "HA!" "Busted his hip if I remember right."

"Now he has to bear some of the responsibility. He could have quit wrestling any time during the night, but NO-OO. He always had to take everything right to the razor's edge."

"And if he'd have stopped, where would we be? Israel would be named Iquit. Nice. We'd have Kuwait, Iran, Iraq, and Iquit." We both laughed until tears welled up.

"No," He said as His laughter subsided. "I'd like to take credit for this pain in your hip, but it's a habit that must be changed."

"I don't think a little ache in my hip and a knot in my shoulder are going to debilitate me," I informed Him. "Do You?"

"It's not the results that concern Me, but the cause. This is because you are stressed. You feel you are under a lot of pressure. Am I wrong?" He asked with the right corner of His mouth turning slightly up. Of course, He wasn't wrong.

"Of course, You're not wrong," I announced with my own slight smile. "It's not hurting now."

"No. The only pain here is the pain I allow, and I see no reason for it at the moment, but it is something you will have to come to terms with. I suggest you start with trusting Me more. Knowing Me is only part of the equation. Understanding Me is the more difficult part of it. You know that I am here, but until you understand the depth of love I have for you, it won't be possible for you to fully trust Me."

"What are You talking about?" My question was voiced with traces of disdain. "I'm here, aren't I? How could You say I need to trust You?"

"Because you're stressed. If you know Me, and you trust Me, what exactly do you have to be stressed about? You trust Me, which by consequence means that you have nothing at all to worry about and no pressure on earth can cause you weariness."

"Drives me nuts when You make sense."

"Would you prefer I fill you with nonsense?"

"Probably." I chuckled. "At least I wouldn't have to be constantly looking for the sense that You ultimately make in what You do. Aren't You going to listen to the old chest pump?" I asked His back while He turned around to pluck something off the table behind Him.

"I already know your heart." He raised His left hand bent at the elbow and worked it into a dark blue latex glove.

My eyes widened noticeably. *This should be interesting.* The thought fired through my mind before I could catch it.

I heard Him softly mumble, "Interesting indeed," before turning back around to face me while snapping the glove over His right hand. As soon as He laced His fingers together, checking the snugness and fit of His rubber gloves, He sank His fingers under my jawline and then searched the point where my tongue and throat intersected above my Adam's apple. He then ran His thumb and first two fingers down either side of my esophagus before pressing lightly at my larynx. "Uh huh" was all He uttered.

The latex was softening the Superman effect that I experienced earlier when He touched me, but it could not abate the sensation completely. The colors and textures and tastes and sparkles danced and intermingled like a gourmet dinner at an IMAX movie theater.

He dropped the large silver reflector from His forehead and positioned it directly in front of His right eye. He then tapped my left cheek with the first two fingers of His right hand. "Open up and let's take a look," He ordered. He ran His thumbs down either side of my tongue and announced, "Oh yeah. There it is. We can take care of this right here." He had a look of promise when He raised the reflector back to its perch on His forehead.

So that's what it's used for, I thought. *To reflect light into the dark places and make them easier to see.* My eyes opened a bit further. "Kayk kahh uh wwhuu?" I asked, as I felt Him pinch the tip of my tongue.

"Take care of this tendency of yours. It's all I want from you on this visit." He began pulling on my tongue. He continued pulling and it continued lengthening until it was roughly the length of my forearm and nearly as big around. He was now easily slipping both hands over the entire length of the slimy surface of the massive protrusion hanging from my mouth. "Just about got it now."

"Mmmm-unmnmmmttt," I protested. Not a word could fit around this moray eel hanging from my mouth. It felt to have roots sunk deep into my chest and whatever it was, He was massaging and pulling and working it completely out of me. "MMM-UUUMMMM!!" I protested louder.

"Easy now. Just about there," He whispered. "Now hold still."

He turned His back to me again, facing the tabletop behind Him. He slipped open the top right drawer and lifted a small dropper bottle and turned back toward me. "Be still," He ordered again. "This might sting a little." He unscrewed the bottle cap and raised the dropper slightly, pinching the rubber nipple sticking up from the cap.

I watched with a growing sense of fear while a dense cloud of condensate oozed from the opened cap of the bottle. He held the dropper directly above the eel-like thing that started out as my tongue, and I watched as three drops were loosed from the rubber nipple, landing directly on the center of this unwelcome mass hanging from my mouth.

It began slowly. The spot where those three drops landed paled instantly and began cracking. The word stinging wasn't even in the neighborhood of descriptors where my mind was living at that moment. Volcanic sun spots of pain flashed through my tongue as the paling cracks spiderwebbed over the entire surface of this thing He pulled out of me. I closed my eyes tightly and surrendered the fight against the molten iron pouring out of my mouth.

"Just about," He said with an intent eye on this thing. I snapped my eyes open at the sound of His voice, tears flooding down my face offering the only outlet for the ferocity of this pain. I had no way of expelling the surge of screams bottling up, and no way to express my objection when I watched Him quickly snatch the reflex hammer from the breast pocket of His smock.

He dropped the hammer sharply onto the hardened, frozen mass, shattering it into a thousand painful shards that dissipated instantly into smoke and rose to the ceiling. The sheer volume of the scream that heaved from my lungs startled even me. I threw my hands up over my ears, fearing my head would explode with the pain. Once I caught my breath, I sobbed deeply.

My tongue was suddenly normal again, aside from a slight tingling. It had returned to its normal size and place, and when I let go of my own face and looked up, He was watching me with sad eyes. "I thought you said there wasn't any pain here!" I said through the shuddering anguish.

"No-o. I said the only pain here is the pain I allow." He corrected.

"Why would you allow that?" I was no longer in pain, but the shock of what had just happened was beginning to give way to anger.

"Some lessons must be painful. In being so, they are not easily forgotten."

"What was that thing?" I asked, a little horrified.

"That, young man, was your tendency to swear. You've mastered the talent, but you have no more need of it."

"But I like to swear. It makes me relatable."

"No. It makes you an idiot. You have also mastered the language, and swearing is fodder. You are more than capable of explaining any point of discussion without the filler of useless wordage. You are much more likely to be heard and your perspective respected if you eliminate the swearing from your vocabulary, and I'm going to need you on your best behavior for an upcoming project."

"What's coming now?" I complained.

"Soon" was all He would say about it. "You did a wonderful job with that young man. Thank you."

I decided not to whine about the reward of having my guts frozen and shattered and left it at "You're welcome." I queried further, "I still have a tongue and an acquired mastery of slang. How does this keep me from swearing?"

"It doesn't," He answered. "It just makes the act a very painful one. You'll see soon enough."

"Hey," I suddenly remembered. "Isn't there more to this place than Your denlibratory?"

"My what?"

"This place. I call it Your denlibratory. How come there aren't any streets of gold and angels and saints and gates and harps? You know. Where is everybody at?"

"You'll have plenty of time to meet the rest later. This is our time. Time for just you and Me to communicate, reflect, meditate, listen... You know...quality time."

"You just finished torturing me. I hardly think that qualifies as quality time. That whole thing was straight out of the bizarro world."

"Understanding does not always fall within your present capacity."

When I raised my eyes toward Him, I was no longer sitting on an examination table. I was seated on a heavily padded leather couch and He was sitting, cross-legged, in an overstuffed armchair with a very high back. He had a flip pad of paper on His knee, taking notes in His bow tie and looking down through His undersized reading glasses. His beard had been shaven down to a thin goatee, and the only thing missing was the meerschaum pipe hanging from the corner of His mouth.

"You're going to make me go back, aren't You?"

"Yez." He had a thick German accent that I found almost comical. "I'm afraid zo. Diz iz joost how it iz done."

"But I don't want to go back," I told Him through the tears welling in my eyes.

He uncrossed His legs and sat up straight, leaning into me. "I know zat." Then He tapped me on the left cheek again and said, "Zat, My zun, iz zee problem."

I closed my eyes against the tears threatening to fall and when I opened them again, the entire room had turned a brilliant, sterile white. From His goatee to His shoes, the walls, the chair He was seated in, to the leather couch upon which I sat, everything became a pristine, fluorescent white. The white digital timer on the stand next to His chair clicked down its final few seconds before pulsing an electronic note to let Him know that my time on the couch had expired. *Dee-dee-deet...dee-dee-deet*, and growing louder, *DEE-DEE-DEET...DEE-DEE-DEET!*

7

HEALING THE DEAF

I.

DEE-DEE-DEET...DEE-DEE-DEET! Cowboy's alarm rudely announced. And again, *DEE-DEE-DEET...DEE-DEE-DEET!*

His head ached as he rolled over, telling the clock on his nightstand to shut up as he slapped at its buttons. He opened one eye at his easterly window and could see light trickling into the morning sky, but the sun had not shown itself yet. Another long day on not nearly enough sleep. It was hard to think over the dull throb pulsing from the back of his head.

He decided to wait until he showered, dressed, and started the day before taking any more of the ibuprofen tablets in the medicine cabinet. "Might just need to get the blood pumping to get rid of that ache." As he brushed his teeth in front of the steamed mirror, he happily noticed the throbbing was barely perceptible.

He stopped at the convenience store on his way out of town and filled his truck with high-octane fuel, filled his travel mug with high-octane coffee, and snatched a PowerBar off the shelf before dropping the truck into gear and heading south. He had a half-dozen inspections he could do to work his way to the University Medical Center before stopping to visit Father Billings.

He spent the next hour uneventfully, wondering how he was

going to approach the priest, certain that he would boot him straight back out the door he entered even before offering him a pleasant greeting. Cowboy could see the suburbs coming to life at the city's edge and changed his thoughts to the first inspection of the day. It was going to be at a dry-cleaners near the north end of town in a small urban strip mall.

He lifted a strip of cinnamon gum from his center console and peeled the tip free of its aluminum wrapper. Poking the tip of the gum between his lips, he slid the wrapper the rest of the way off and crumpled it, balling it between his thumb and finger and dropping it where it started on the truck console.

Cowboy looked up just in time to see a UTV cruising down his shoulder of the road. Distance, weight, and speed differentials were all thoughts that immediately focused on the equation of avoiding a collision. The UTV was too big to fit entirely within the boundaries of the highway's shoulder, and too slow to maintain the sixty miles per hour speed limit.

Cowboy slammed his brakes against two oncoming cars filling the other lane of this two-laner. The thought of putting his truck through the barbed-wire fence and into the cornfield sprawled out to his right made him stomp the brake pedal down even further. *If I even make it down the embankment without flipping this rig,* he thought as the camouflaged rear of the UTV grew dangerously close, *my whole front end is going to be completely wiped out by the fencing.*

With a burst of speed, the UTV managed to stay in front of Cowboy's truck and he wrestled it back off the shoulder, into his lane, and safely back behind the recreational vehicle doing a full-out thirty-five miles an hour. Now Cowboy was growing furious at the stupidity of the two men in the UTV. The two oncoming cars flashed by and Cowboy started feverishly gnawing on his cinnamon gum, thinking of exactly what he was going to bellow when he passed these idiots.

With the passing lane clear, he rolled down the passenger window and began working his way around the UTV. He could see two bow cases strapped to the back bed and neither of the two young bowmen were wearing helmets, but the doors were on and they were well buttoned up inside their little camouflaged Polaris Ranger. Cowboy was going to have to give this one all he was worth to be heard. He leaned toward the open window and screamed, "You ignorant sons-a b… OOOWWWWW!"

Cowboy threw his cupped hand over his mouth, muffling the sound of his own whimpering. It the midst of gnawing his cinnamon gum and bellowing at the two bow hunters, he bit the tip of his tongue nearly off. *OH MY GOD!* he screamed inside his head. *OH MY GOD that hurts!* He could taste the blood filling his mouth. He rolled down his window and spat the cinnamon gum and blood down the side of his truck.

I've got to pull over at the next gas station, he thought. The only thing that could make biting his tongue so hard worse would be to have a mouthful of fresh cinnamon flavoring at the time. He spat out his window again before rolling both windows up and spotting a BP convenience store and pulling in.

He immediately went into the men's restroom and stood facing the mirror with his tongue poked out at his reflection. A horribly painful tear just past the left side of the tip informed him that he probably didn't need any stitches, but it took several flushes with cold water to stop the bleeding. He filled his go cup with ice as he left the store, nodding at the sunflower seeds on his way by. *Don't foresee any of those in the near future, ya genius,* he thought, but he didn't smile at all and his face was still red with pain.

II.

As he climbed back into his truck, he dumped a mouthful of ice from his travel mug into his cheek and poked his sore tongue into it. He could still taste the blood, but the ice was blissfully welcome and he held it there for as long as he could stand the cold. By the time he had reached his first inspection, he had the pain and bleeding under control and the color of his face returned to normal.

The completion of his fourth inspection found him turning up

University Avenue not ten blocks from the medical center. He still had no idea what he would say to the priest when he pulled into the parking garage and locked the doors. *Guess I'll just have to wing it*, he decided after strolling to the information desk.

"I'm here to see Father Charles Billings," he told the elderly woman behind the help desk.

"Well, isn't he Mr. Popularity this morning." She smiled. "A whole group of staff members just left his room not ten minutes ago. They brought him all kinds of things he's not allowed to have and then they prayed together. Must have been a dozen of them in there laughing and talking this morning," she informed Cowboy. She seemed genuinely happy for the visitors Father Billings had, having seen too many others here who had no visitors at all. "You'll find him up in room six eighteen."

Cowboy punched the big blue six in the glass elevator and watched the people milling about the lobby zoom out as he ascended. He strode down the east wing until he found a door half opened with the three black numbers posted at eye level. He pushed the door the rest of the way open and stepped in, and the priest's eyes turned to meet his.

"You? What the hell are you doing here, you..." the priest paused, searching for a finish to his thought, "you damn wild man?" He was hollering at Cowboy in that growling, raspy voice. Cowboy found the texture of that voice unnerving. It seemed to be filled with intellect and a frustrated curiosity.

Probably left with the unanswered question of 'why' too many times, Cowboy thought. *I just can't figure out why he's so angry and yelling at me.* "Well, I was in the neighborhood and..." Cowboy was interrupted by a pretty young nurse pushing her way through the door and past him. Cowboy read the pin on her lapel. It simply said, "Morgan RN."

"The batteries are gone again," she told the priest.

"What? What are you saying?" Father Billings looked at her with confusion.

She pointed to her right ear and yelled, "The batteries in your hearing aids are gone again. Here," she reached into the pocket of her smock, "I brought you some fresh ones. Let me help you put them in." She spoke so loudly that even she sounded frustrated. She reached up to either side of his head and began fiddling with his hearing devices. They were small flesh-toned inserts that were difficult to manipulate, but she had them back in place in no time at all.

"How's that?" she asked in a casual tone. "Better?"

The priest reached up and slid his arm around her, planting his hand in the center of her back. "My God," he announced. "You could be sanctified. You've cured an old man of his deafness. Soon enough, we'll find out if you can raise one from the dead." He laughed as she pulled the priest's ear against her breast and hugged his head. "Thank you, my love," he told her, and she kissed him on the top of his head, turned, and marched past Cowboy and out of the room, wiping a tear from her right cheek.

"Holy sh... OH!" Cowboy winced when the *sh* brought his tongue against the roof of his mouth. He cupped his hand over his mouth again, squeezed his eyes against the pain, and shook his head a little. *That hurt*, he warned himself. *Let's keep those syllables in mind as we proceed. This looks to be more of a listening encounter and less of a talking one.*

Still, he was stunned at the revelation: The priest wasn't angry with him at all. He couldn't hear well and did not have his hearing aids in during their first encounter. He wasn't yelling at him any more than he was barking at the nurse just now.

The priest had gone back to looking out his hospital room window exactly as Cowboy had found him when he entered the room. "I helped that young lady find Christ when she was working nights during my first round of treatments," he told no one. Then he snapped his gaze back into focus and turned it directly at Cowboy. "What on God's green earth are you doing here? I've got people who actually like me coming to visit and need not sour my mood on the likes of you."

"So I've heard," Cowboy told him. "I think we've had some sort of misunderstanding..."

The priest threw his right forearm up and pointed toward the ceiling. "I wouldn't call me Padre again, unless you want to bear the lifelong humiliation of having a sick old man kick the crap out of you."

"No, sir," Cowboy responded. "I believe you mentioned your disapproval previously. No. I suspect I've been the victim of a mis-understanding for nearly a year now, having spoken with you last winter and frequently recollecting our conversation since. I was afraid I made you angry with our discussion."

The priest sat with a furrowed brow behind his unbelievably thick glasses. His own parental patience kept him from asking his question again, but he crossed his arms and waited for this joker to finish blathering.

"Uh," Cowboy stammered, "I'm here to...well...I thought you were angry with me and I heard you had taken ill, so I thought..." Cowboy had no way of knowing how to finish the thoughts stutter-ing through his mind.

"It's simply a matter of perspective," Father Billings offered in relief to the nerves shown by Cowboy. "I'm not mad. I'm too old to be mad anymore. I've had to let too many things go to be mad anymore. So many things..."

"What do you mean a matter of perspective?" Cowboy asked, wincing a little as his tongue seemed to slam against his palate with every *t* spoken.

"Perspective. Everything is about the conveyance of perspec-tive. Listen," he commanded. "Within your perspective you thought I was angry, and for a year now you've stewed on it, building in frustration and recollecting the manner in which you thought you were being treated. My lovely nurse comes in and simply puts a new pair of ears on me and voila, your entire perspective changed. Such a simple act allowed your perspective to change from one of frustration over my deafness to one of appreciation over my ability to read lips."

"You handled me throughout our entire conversation." Cowboy was shocked. "You played that entire conversation through before you ever even asked me what I think."

"Almost. I admit to being surprised at your conclusion that man, at his most elemental, is good. It is not at all what I've concluded, but after listening to you, I tried on your perspective to see if it fit, and honestly, I couldn't find any holes in it."

"Are you saying I may be right?" Cowboy showed Father Billings a short smile.

"I'm saying you may be right, but you're not hearing me, and you aren't even wearing electronic ears. HA!" He guffawed in a raspy, familiar way. "Come over here and sit for a minute. My glasses don't reach as far as they used to and I want to see your face."

Cowboy slid the unpadded cafeteria chair next to the bed and sat as Father Billings continued.

"This refusal to consider another's perspective, to admit the possibility that we could be wrong, this is the root of all conflict on the planet. It is the unfulfillable desire to be unique amongst the human race. It's what causes world wars all the way down to bar brawls and divorce."

"I can't disagree with that," Cowboy admitted. "Nor can I resolve it. It is the infinity loop of equations. Everyone wants to be special, if only by their perspective. But of course, if everyone is special, that means that no one is."

"That's right. The problem with perspective is that, in order to fully acquire and appreciate another perspective, you have to fully surrender your own. It is absolute fear that prevents us from doing that because of the question 'what if I'm wrong?' It is that question that forces us to try desperately to fit in. We wear what is fashionable and buy cars that are popular and use phones that are state-of-the-art. That way, we can say that if we are wrong, so was everyone else. See?"

"What I see, Professor," Cowboy stated with a serious look directly into the priest's glasses, "is six point eight billion of us destroying the planet in the hopes of finding acceptance in our unique popularity. You, of course, can see the insanity of it."

"Yes," the priest almost hissed in agreement. "You see that basic contradiction. But, can you see something more? Let me show you something. " Father Billings looked as if he was actually going to manifest something tangible to show Cowboy, when in fact, he was gesturing to expose an idea. "Christ tells us that *narrow is the way that leads unto life.*"

Cowboy added, "The Katha Upanishads tell us that *narrow is the way that leads to light, as narrow as the razor's edge.*"

"I asked the universe why is the path so narrow? If God loves all His children, then why is the path to righteousness so narrow?"

"Woo," Cowboy offered. "Good question."

"I discovered it is a matter of perspective. Have you ever seen those extreme up-close photographs in magazines where they ask you to figure out what it is you are looking at? It could be a fly's eye, or a butterfly's wing, or a leopard's spots. Do you know what I mean? They take an extremely close picture of it and ask you to figure out what it is. I'm usually pretty good at it when my eyes are working right, but when I can't come up with the answer and I have to look it up, I think, *Of course that's what it is. How could I have not seen it?* Right?"

"Yeah." Cowboy had seen these pictures in children's magazines. "Those are actually kind of fun."

"What if," the priest continued in anticipation, "what if the narrow path is only narrow because of our perspective? What if we use extreme close-up photography to look at the path again? If we magnify the edge of a razor, we can make it look like a four-lane highway. See what I mean?"

"I do," Cowboy admitted. "But how do we magnify the path?"

"We don't, young man." The priest touched Cowboy on the cheek in a familiar, understanding way. "We don't magnify the path. We diminish ourselves. By making ourselves so much smaller..."

"We automatically make the path larger," Cowboy finished quietly. "It is perspective. With the correct perspective, we could bring anyone we wanted with us to walk the path." The image of his father, brought into his mind, started to moisten Cowboy's eyes. "But how do we make ourselves that small?"

"Through a continuous state of servitude and forgiveness. We know the pain of seeking and offering forgiveness, particularly when neither is deserved. We understand servitude toward those who neither appreciate or acknowledge it, but once forgiven, we come to recognize how small we are and how little we can do as individuals."

With his hand on the side of Cowboy's face, the priest added, "He came to us as one of us, and He washed our feet," causing the tears to streak down the apple of Cowboy's cheeks. "He could not have diminished Himself more than that." He then tapped Cowboy on the left cheek in a very familiar way and said, "Go over to that closet and in the right pocket of my trousers you'll find my rosary. Get if for me, will you?"

"Of course." Cowboy began wiping his face on the sleeve of his shirt and coughing lightly at the lump in his throat. He stepped to the closet, reached into the priest's trousers, and pulled out an enormous loop of rosary beads. Handing them to Father Billings, he sat back down next to the bed.

Father Billings turned the crucifix of the rosary over and examined the back of it carefully. He popped a wedge out of the bottom and slid the back panel off. Inside the rosary was a key with the head filed down so that it would fit inside the hollowed-out back of the crucifix. Father Billings held up the key in front of Cowboy's astonished face. "Don't get too excited. It's not for you."

"Who's it for?"

"A student of mine. A young fellow from Texas that I find to be most extraordinary."

"Jason," Cowboy said, smiling. "I found him to be extraordinary as well. In fact, we met just last night." He did not tell him that Jason and his classmates would be there soon, in case it was a surprise.

"It's a key to a safe deposit box at Union Bank. The box is number seven fourteen," the priest instructed.

"Matthew 7:14: *but small is the gate and narrow the road that leads to life.*" Cowboy smiled.

"The box contains the last forty years of my writings and I want Jason to have them, but he's not ready. I want you to collect them now and give them to him as a graduation gift."

"Can I read them?"

"You're not ready yet either," the priest told him, "but I can't stop you. You, of course, can't share them with anyone, not that you would want to, but these are for young Jason."

"Mind if I ask a few questions?" Cowboy's gaze at Father Billings softened in understanding. He knew the priest had no intention of surviving the treatments he faced. Cowboy nodded at the hospital room and the equipment surrounding Father Billings. "Why all this?"

"This is for show. I'm ready to go home. I welcome the thought, but the people I'm leaving behind need to know that I loved them so much that I would fight to my last breath and endure any torture to stay with them. And I have every intention of expending that last breath by telling them so."

"Why me?"

The priest looked him in the eye. "You're not swayed by religious fervor or iconography. Your belief is set in the concreteness of understanding. It has solidity and is not easily shaken. Like most of us, you're not afraid to ask the great questions. Unlike most of us, you're not afraid of the answers you get. Aristotle said that a life un-examined is not worth living, but it was Descartes who taught that the act of examining your life is not for the weak-minded. Plus," he added, "you're not a complete idiot." That caused a wide grin to spread across both their faces.

"I appreciate that," Cowboy said. "So, why Jason?"

"I'm not exactly sure, or I'm not ready to say. Gut feeling maybe. You say you met him last night. What was your take?" the priest asked.

"He's brilliant."

"Far brighter than both of us put together when we were twice his age. He has a faith and understanding that I find remarkable. He has a capacity to serve and an ability to forgive... even El Diablo." The priest's voice faded to a reflective whisper at the end of his as-sessment, but then picked up its volume again. "Who knows what he can do and where he can go. Maybe he's the next Pope, or will ring in the second coming."

"Or maybe he's the antichrist," Cowboy added, deciding to leave the priest's whispering reference to El Diablo alone.

"That's what I like about you. You're not afraid to try on any perspective just to see how it fits. Maybe he is. God knows, and in either case, shouldn't we do what we can to let His will be done?" Father Billings had a point. "I think these scribblings of mine might help him gain a little perspective of his own."

"I'll see to it that he gets them, Father." It was the first time in all of their encounters that Cowboy referred to him as father. While he did not much care for referring to anyone as father, Cowboy was surprised how well it sounded in his own voice. "You have my word on that."

"I believe that," the priest confirmed. "Now get out of here. I have people who actually like me coming to visit."

"So you already know about the visitors?"

"Of course. You said you met Jason on the return flight from Houston. Why else would he be on that flight nearly a week before the break ends? You really are slow-witted." The priest laughed at the figure standing above him now, tucking the key he'd received neatly into his wallet.

"It was a real pleasure meeting you, Father," Cowboy said, taking the priest's hand. Despite his age and condition, Father Billings' hand was solid and rugged. *The hand of a soldier*, Cowboy thought.

"You can call me Chuck," Father Billings allowed.

"Well, Chuck, I can't say I've ever met anyone more fascinating. Mind if I make a return visit when I'm back in town?"

"Only if I can't talk you out of it," the priest guffawed.

"No chance of that." Cowboy was laughing with him.

"I guess I'll either be here," he paused, "or I won't," he finished, laughing again.

Cowboy gave the father's hand a single firm pump in spite of the tubes that hung from it. "Thanks, Chuck."

"My pleasure, sir."

Cowboy spun and strolled toward the door. Just outside the doorway was Morgan, Father Billings' nurse. She had her hands laced behind her back listening to the tail end of the conversation, and when Cowboy entered the hall, he nearly bumped into her.

She stood looking up at Cowboy with a deeply saddened expression hidden just behind her eyes. She knew the priest was not long for the world. "It's going to be okay," Cowboy informed her. "He's ready."

"But I'm not," she said with a tear starting to form at the bottom of her eye.

Cowboy snapped one of his business cards out of his shirt pocket and poked it at the nurse. "Yes, you are," he told her, "because it is going to happen." She unlaced her fingers and reached out to take the card. She didn't expect to find comfort in Cowboy's explanation, but he said it so matter-of-factly that it was comforting. She was ready; she had no choice but to be so. "Here is my contact information. If that man needs anything at all, will you please be so kind as to let me know?"

"Of course," she said and watched Cowboy as he stepped toward the glass elevators.

While Cowboy walked toward the parking garage, he could see through his dark sunglasses that his path was going to be crossed by a group of a half-dozen young men. He recognized Jason as one of them.

"Hey!" Jason yelled. "Hey, you guys, come here." He turned to offer his companions a wave of encouragement. "This is the guy I was telling you about this morning. Hey!" Jason threw out his hand to the approaching Cowboy. "I got your email this morning," he said while firmly shaking hands.

"Good deal." Cowboy smiled. "Glad we could connect."

"Hey, you guys," Jason said over his shoulder. "This is the fella I was telling you about. The guy I met on the plane last night."

One of his classmates pulled his sunglasses down to the tip of his nose with his index finger. "This is the wild man?" he asked with a hint of disdain while peeking over the frames, as if he expected so much more than just this.

"Yeah. Yeah. This is him," Jason confirmed with a mild excitement.

"Hey. You must have come to visit Father Billings. How is he?"

"He's doing great," Cowboy lied. "He's really looking forward to seeing you guys."

"Oh man! You told him we were coming? We were going to surprise him," one young man complained.

"Absolutely not. I didn't say a word, but did you guys think for one minute that he doesn't know what you're up to all the time? Randy," Cowboy pointed to the young man with the pack half slung over his shoulder, "how often does Father Billings speak to your mother up there in Boston?"

The boys all had a mildly stunned expression when they turned toward Randy. "At least twice a week. She calls him all the time."

"There, you see?" Cowboy smiled at them all. "I don't have to tell him what you're up to. He surely knows already." He nodded at the crowd and patted Jason firmly on the shoulder. "Great to see you again. I want you to stay in touch, now. I mean it. I've got to run though. Enjoy your visit with the father."

All of the boys were looking with the same stunned expression at Cowboy as he walked away, except for Jason. Jason was staring at Randy until he finally noticed the name tag on his shoulder pack. The information on it was handwritten in a woman's cursive and included his name and phone number, with, of course, a Boston area code. Jason didn't say a word to his classmates as they finally turned and quick paced it toward the hospital's front entry.

8

BACK TO THE BEGINNING

I.

Cowboy completed two more inspections before Mike called to let him know the dates for his pending visit to Abu Dhabi. Everyone at that end of the investigation was geared up for a Sunday visit, which meant Cowboy had to be on a flight first thing Friday morning. He texted Christy to let her know where he was going and when, and when he expected to return. They were going to pick him up at the airport in Dubai, so no car was needed, and she knew the rest regarding preferred airlines and hotels. Cowboy was looking forward to the trip since he hadn't been to the Middle East in a long time.

He made his last inspection of the day, which was coincidentally only a few blocks from the Union Bank. He strolled into the front doors and asked to have access to the safe deposit boxes. A very neatly dressed, middle-aged woman of small stature and wide smile was more than willing to help him into the room with the walls lined with numbered panels. Cowboy lifted the key from his wallet and turned the lock on the panel numbered 714.

He was surprised at the depth of the box he slid out from behind the panel. It looked to be nearly three feet long and eight inches deep when he set it on the table in the center of the room.

There were eleven identical leather-bound composition notebooks in four neat columns, with three in the first three stacks and two in the fourth. The elaborately tooled leather covers were bound shut with the leather latigo provided. Each appeared well cared for, but well-worn, and the smell of old leather filled Cowboy's nose as he lifted each one carefully out of the box.

They all fit into his rucksack, and he slid the box back behind its panel before locking it. He returned to the same teller behind the counter and asked if he could cancel the lease on the box. She gave him a brief form to sign and examined the deformed key, trying to decide what to do with it. "If you could just give me one minute to confer with our branch manager, I'll be right back," she told him while stepping around the counter and walking to the glass-front offices to her left.

Cowboy could see the manager sneering at the key and wondering how it got to be that way, when he handed it back to the teller, shaking his head from side to side. The teller returned to her post and informed him that there would be a charge for the replacement of the key. Cowboy nodded politely and gave the teller twenty-two dollars, thinking, *Pretty steep for a silly key.* He spent the next ninety minutes wondering what the old priest had written in these tomes while making the late afternoon drive home. He was exhausted from the day's work, the emotional visit with the priest, and the lack of sleep from the night before. He couldn't remember the last time he had looked so forward to getting home.

He walked through his front door and returned his pack to the side panel hook of the bookcase where he had collected it on his way out that morning. He glanced over the books filling the wall. Their content ranged from equipment technical manuals to philosophy to religion to business to just about everything else under the sun, with the exception of politics. Cowboy had a sharp disdain for politics and believed all men should learn to govern themselves.

Retrieving the manuals that Father Billings had written, he stacked them in two piles of five, with the eleventh book centered at the top of the pile. The priest had even labeled them as Volume I through Volume XI, and the top of the stack was the first of the series. He found the father's ability to amass such a quantity of ideas extremely impressive. *It could take some time to chew through all of this*, he thought, *but I would bet my last silver dollar it's worth it.*

He showered and brushed his teeth, having already had his usual fare at Maddie's Diner on the way home. It was good to see Maddie and she seemed genuinely happy to sit and visit with Cowboy while he ate and she sipped her coffee. She always appeared interested in where he had been in the world, and where he was planning on going next. "I've got to fly out to Abu Dhabi at the end of the week," he had told her.

"Abu Dhabi? I didn't even think that was a real place." She laughed. "It sounds like something made up from the Aladdin stories. Do you suppose there are still forty thieves hanging around there in some dark alley?" She laughed again through a raspy smoker's hack. Although she had quit smoking two years earlier, the effects were clear.

Cowboy enjoyed Maddie's company and sense of humor for the better part of an hour, and she was an excellent cook to boot. His thoughts fell back on the writings he collected earlier that day as he stood in front of his desk and lifted Volume I off the top of the stack. He untied the latigo and examined the title page. *"In the beginning..."* was written in black ink across the center of the page. At the bottom right corner, it acknowledged *"C. R. Billings."*

At first, Cowboy presumed the priest had formulated a biblical dissertation that started at Genesis, but when he flipped the page, he realized how wrong he was. This was where Father Billings began his search for God—directly in the Song Gianh River valley in Vietnam as part of the 137th Marine regiment:

This was not my first encounter with raw violence, but where I started chronicling the experience of war. My first encounter ended in an eight-week stay at the medical unit. I couldn't get out of it because of that damned broken rib. Captain's orders. But, while I was there, I met up with a Navy corpsman that was tough as boot leather, had three years of med school, and wanted nothing more than to be in the fray of blood and beer and combat. He was tagged with the name Willow when he stitched his own wound after an artillery round hit the tree behind him. A large chunk of the tree flew off and hit him square under the left shoulder blade, which he immediately extracted and, using a field mirror, cleaned and sutured the wound himself. One look at this gangly squid, and it was clear that he was as flexible as a wet belt and twice as tough.

Cowboy blinked hard two times against the blurring weariness that the end of the day brought. His stomach swirled with nausea, which, he thought, would be expected when reading a chronicle of war. He knew war was a product of government, and that government was man's attempt at creating God, as had been proven throughout the history of every failed civilization. Civilization fails because it insists on being governed. Those civilizations currently existing had just not yet failed, but he knew they would in their attempt to carve God out of the earth. War was the chisel used; war under the guise of freedom, birthright, fortune, Democracy, Communism, and worst of all, under the guise of God. He continued his reading.

My first taste of savagery was ended by a preadolescent with a grenade. MPs were Jeeping it to where me and my platoon were enjoying our passes while waiting assignment. My platoon of thirty-two men was a mongrel batch, mostly out of Texas, with thirty of the thirty-two of Mexican heritage, and all fluent in Spanish.

As the MPs rolled up to where I was planted on a short stack of pallets soaking in the warm sun after a fresh morning rain, this kid bolted out from an alley, and either not knowing what he was doing, or overly zealous in his mission, he had already pulled the pin. The grenade reached the top of its arc before I realized what was happening, and exploded immediately upon landing in the box of the Jeep. The ass end of the vehicle jumped straight up, but when the boy tossing it stopped, he lost his footing in the mud and slid on his ass toward the half airborne rig. I instinctually threw my right arm up to cover and spun to the left toward the sensation of hot iron hitting me under my left nipple, watching the scene unfold in ultra-slow motion. The back end of the Jeep came whomping back to the ground, bouncing twice and pinning the boy's foot under the rear passenger tire.

I had been in plenty of fights as a kid, but this was real; this was defining. I placed my right hand under my left breast pocket, felt my cheroot cigars and Zippo lighter still there and the hole left by the single fragment of shrapnel. I smelled the cloth still smoking and looked at my blood smeared across the tips of my fingers, and as I surveyed the scene, could feel the raw fury welling within. I felt no pain, heard no sound, and watched my men scurry out the fronts of the bars and brothels. I couldn't even hear myself when I barked for Jasper, my medic at the time, to get the MPs out. He was standing barefoot under the makeshift canopy over the walk in his white T-shirt still fumbling with his belt while gawking at the two men in the Jeep.

The driver had caught a single large piece of shrapnel behind his left ear, and as I watched Jasper pull his slumping body off the steering wheel, we all knew he had no more life in him than a store mannequin. Although the passenger MP's back was shredded, he was still pumping air in a bubbling, gurgling sound that held his screaming to a low, awful growl. His seat cushion had suffered the brunt of the blast and I thought he might have a chance, until Jasper pulled the fuel-soaked medic bag from under the seat. Jasper was desperately patching him together. Both lungs were punctured and his lower spine broken by the concussion of the explosion, but Jasper's saddened head shaking told me the soldier was taking his last breath.

The amazing thing was that the ten-gallon fuel can strapped to the box of the Jeep ruptured, throwing gasoline all over the immediate area, but it hadn't ignited. Most of my men were scrambling around the vehicle sorting themselves and the debris field out as I showed Jasper the palm of my hand when he took a step toward me with a handful of bandages. He saw me wince sharply when I purposefully stood and filled my lungs to capacity, and I was letting him know I was going to be fine for the moment. My lung was not punctured, but I knew the gash would need stitching and there was at least one broken rib below it, and pain that followed fueled the growing rage.

The noise of the situation finally found its way to my ears. There were only a few brave bystanders who had not fled the scene, and most of the men had formed a haphazard circle with weapons in hand feverishly looking about for any sign of additional danger. The sound of a distant, honking siren of the local police or an ambulance that was making its way closer was subdued by the squealing of the boy viciously pulling at his own ankle, trying to free his foot from under the Jeep's tire. He was soaked by the contents of the ruptured fuel can.

There was no sane voice in me that was needed to quell the peaking fury, and I slowly approached the kid, pulled a cheroot and the Zippo from my pocket, and lit it. I stood above that boy with the lighter still aflame and dropped it directly into his lap. That earned me the nickname El Diablo, and also the high-pitched, haunting screams of that boy that I endured every day since.

His sour stomach worsened, and Cowboy gulped hard to the metallic taste forming in his mouth. He had experienced military conflict before, but nothing this personal. He squinted against his blurring vision and continued.

With eight weeks to heal a ridiculous broken rib and nothing to do being surrounded by the MASH unit's bumbling ground pounders, I struck up a conversation with the corpsman sitting next to me wearing the same unbearably bored stare on his face—Willow. Even the unit's doctors admitted they couldn't have done a better job suturing his wound had they been directly facing it, so they simply left it alone, but because he suffered the same broken rib, he too was looking at six more weeks of uselessness.

He told me that a few of the higher ranking personnel had made several attempts toward convincing him his service would be better spent at the unit, being an enlisted man with such a unique skill set, but he wanted no part of it. I also knew that after the fray in town and the look on his face when I dropped that lighter, Jasper had had his fill of frontline combat medic duty. I spent the next six weeks pulling strings, calling in favors, bribing and blackmailing everyone I needed to get Willow assigned to my platoon and Jasper's orders to the MASH unit. Willow's philosophy was that he would rather be covered in the blood of a single soldier he cared about than a dozen a day that he didn't even know. His explanation was much more eloquent, saying he did not want to feel the obsolescence of his fellow fighting men, only to realize his own.

With the transfers of the two medics complete, and the two of us being released for full active duty within a day of each other, I escorted Willow back to my platoon upon his release and made introductions. Jasper looked immeasurably relieved to be reporting to the MASH unit, but Jasper was very young and had little foresight of the horrors before him. My men were also relieved after hearing the tales of how Willow patched himself up and stayed in the fray, but none of them ever looked at me the same way, using only weary, hesitant glances for eye contact, with the exception of Master Sergeant Connor McCullum.

Culley was my right hand and the only Caucasian left in my outfit, save for the new addition of Willow.

Culley was the iconic Marine. He accepted no hesitation and no excuse when issuing orders, taking an idealistic patriotism and honing it to a scalpel-sharp killing machine through three tours of the worst Korea had to offer, and teaching his men to do the same. He had a hidden admiration for what I did to that boy, and was almost thankful I spared him the task of throwing a lighter himself, because he was fumbling in his pocket for his own trusty Zippo at the time. After I did that, he knew I would lead into any battlefield with a ferocity that matched his own. After I did that, I knew he would follow.

We received orders from Major Redding that afternoon. The major was a soft-spoken, highly intelligent officer who didn't like the orders he issued, but he issued them just the same. When I took Culley to the briefing, I could tell he didn't like them either, but would follow them just the same. This was a different kind of war. It had no sides and no identifiable front. Orders were three adjacent platoons, each in a V pattern, would punch through this river valley, destroy every weapon, burn every supply cache, and kill every communist in it. We were to assemble and dispatch an hour before sunrise with my platoon dead center of the push.

Culley and I gathered the men later that afternoon to convey the day's orders. They looked clean and rested, loosely gathered playing poker, drinking beer, checking their gear, and getting to know Willow better. Culley told them to get off their asses, finish drinking their formaldehyde, and listen up. The two squad leaders, Rodriguez and Mendez, were front and center, and as always, fully dressed, fully sober, and listening intently. Culley told them that first squad would take the left wing, second secured the right, leaving me, Culley, and Willow in the center with three men covering our flank. This valley was steeply sided, covered in a hundred and sixty-seven miles of the planet's ugliest jungle, and as a long-range reconnaissance force, we were about to take a fifteen-mile bite out of it in the next twelve days of humping.

We were assigned a South Vietnamese interpreter that morning, an Army regular that made our recon men look like Girl Scouts. He lived in the field, fought through bouts of dysentery and malaria, and couldn't have weighed ninety pounds, but every ounce of that was driven by his single, contented sense of purpose. My men took one look at him and started handing him cans of field rations and cigarettes, which he accepted with a smile and quick bow of his head in thanks. His name was Quahn Duc, and he spoke in a loud, raspy nasal voice. The men immediately tagged him with the nickname Quack. He would be planted in the center of the V formation with me, carrying an old, fully functional, and well-worn World War Two vintage Tommy gun, and at least a dozen fifty-round banana clips on his belt. His gear looked to outweigh him, but no one doubted his ability to carry it.

As was Culley's habit, he offered me the good news and bad news of the situation. Good news was that humping should be easier through the center, since that was where the trails and roads were carved out of the brush. The bad news was, of course, that this was where most of the population was located. Five helicopters lit out an hour before sunrise and dropped us in a cleared patch in an overgrown trench slashed into the earth's surface. It looked like a kill box; like a badly healed surgery scar hacked into the earth's crust with a dull hatchet. We stagger-stepped up the widened trail as the sun rose since there was no way any of the three platoons could keep formation in the narrowness of the valley, and it was a full three hours before encountering a small assembly of maybe a dozen huts.

The men formed a semicircle as we entered the small village, with Culley barking orders to clear every building and gather the *indigs*, what we called the indigenous people, in the patch near the center. Culley himself cleared the first and largest building, informing me that there was an older man and a younger couple, one boy of about six years old, the woman pregnant with a baby on her hip. This little two-room hut would be a good interrogation center, and as I entered, I could see there was a room for sleeping, and a larger room for everything else. Against the far wall of the larger room was a small table draped in a long blue cloth with a bench against the wall and two chairs parked neatly at the front of it. As I sat on the bench with my back against the wall facing the doorway, I told Culley, who was standing in it and scowling at the two men, to fetch Quack. The vicious little bastard couldn't wait to join the left squad of riflemen to help clear huts, and Culley was all for the idea of getting him off the task to minimize the chance of any shooting.

On the floor near the adjacent wall to my left was a three-piece cooking stand with a small straw fire under the large cookpot filled with steaming rice. It smelled good and it was the first I had realized how hungry I was. The younger and older men moved the chairs against the wall to the right and stood in front of the table facing me. Knowing it was futile, I asked if anyone spoke English while waiting for Quack to show. These people were poor, malnourished, and disgruntled.

The younger of the two men began talking, speaking quickly in a high-pitched rambling manner. I could only understand the word "American," sounding much like "Ammican," and as the volume of his voice raised, he suddenly reached under the table cloth, yanking the leg of the table up in a twirling fashion, which happened to be a Mosin-Nagant M91 Dragoon rifle. In ultra-slow motion, I instinctually threw my right hand up to cover and, again, could not hear or feel anything except my own heartbeat.

The gun went off as I dove for cover between the bench and the now sagging tabletop. I watched the tip of my pinky finger seem to jump off my hand at the second knuckle as the bullet passed through it and down the side of my right cheek, taking a piece of my earlobe off as it smashed into the wall behind me. I had reached for my M1911 holstered to my right leg while falling to the floor, having only enough time for it to take the young man to open the bolt and jack another round into the barrel of the Soviet-made rifle. The older of the two was still tugging at the second table leg made from an identical rifle. I could see the lip of the table was jammed against the butt of the rifle, keeping him from getting it free.

I was so close to them it required no aim for me to shoot the younger man in both knees, swinging quickly enough to see the older man jump at the report of my pistol, and sending one into his right knee. The younger man's rifle clattered to the floor across the room when he dropped. The older man dropped with both hands covering his right kneecap, having never gotten his out from under the table. I heard the fourth round of my forty-five drown out the shrieking of the pregnant woman with the boy hiding behind her. We were lying on the floor facing each other when the bullet passed through the young man's left eye and slammed into the door frame behind him, where I could see Quack's sandals arriving and jumping to the side, away from the sound of the bullet hitting the wood. He emptied his Thompson into everyone left standing in the room and quickly, before the woman's, the boy's, and the baby's bodies splashed to the floor, Quack had slapped another clip in his rifle and was standing on the old man's neck. He was screaming at the old man in his raspy, high-pitched Vietnamese, presumably telling him to stay put, with the hot barrel of his Thompson against the older man's temple. I heard Culley's boots clumping quickly through the door.

As I rose off the floor and saw Culley gawking at the scene, we both knew instantly that mistakes in clearing the building were made, and the anger that smeared across his expression when I stood told me that Culley realized he was the one who made them. We both learned the difference between looking under the table and looking at the table. We both learned that a large pot of steaming rice was enough to feed fifteen of these scrawny farmers, not just the five that were in the hut. We learned a terrible lot in those few moments, and in those that followed, we learned where every tunnel hiding the VC soldiers was dug. I ordered Culley to get Willow and brace the men, feeling the blood trickle down my forearm and neck. I knew Willow would do a field patch on me well enough to keep me going. Willow pumped me full of morphine and sewed the gash along the right side of my face and the missing end of my finger. I wouldn't be wasting any more time at the MASH unit, and I sure as hell didn't need any more Purple Hearts.

Sergeant Mendez posted five men around the gathered villagers, hog-tying them and holding them at gunpoint. On my orders, the rest of the men torched every standing structure in the village and every grain of rice stored, shooting the enemy soldiers as they ran out of the flames whether they had their hands raised or not. I could hear Quack laughing and singing "God Bless America" between the short bursts of his Thompson as he killed flaming soldiers.

Still buzzing from the morphine and with Culley now apologetically guarding me like a mother hen, I told Quack to quit singing. God was not here, and if He were not here, then He couldn't be everywhere; and if He were not everywhere, then He was not God. I could only conclude that this ubiquitous, all-loving God did not exist, but the nickname El Diablo was now cemented among the men. Culley looked up the gorge as he barked for the radioman to order support from the adjacent platoon. We both knew that the rising smoke and echoing gunfire would serve to warn the entire valley that we were here, and we brought hell with us.

II:

Cowboy awoke, lifting his face off the open volume he'd been reading at his desk earlier. He noticed saliva laced with blood from the bite on his tongue had stained one of the pages. His eyes blurred out of focus as he shut the leather binder and placed it neatly back on the stack he collected from the safe deposit box earlier that morning. He looked at the G-Shock strapped snugly against his wrist. It informed him it was nearly 2:00 a.m. and he reached for the aching knot on the back of his head, which was pulsing now, trying to push his eyes out of their sockets. "Guess I got them yesterday morning," he said to no one.

As he rose, his nausea returned and brought a sudden bout of dizziness with it that he couldn't control. The lump at the base of his skull had swollen to the size of a duck egg and he braced himself by leaning his right hip heavily against the desk. He staggered to the bathroom and squinted hard against the bright, painful light that invaded the room when he flicked the switch. He pushed his eyes back with his thumb and forefinger, convincing himself that he just needed some rest, and promptly vomited into the toilet. It was the first time he considered the possibility that he might need a doctor to look at his head.

He haphazardly brushed his teeth and flopped into bed on top of the covers, sleeping like a stone through the entire night. He lifted his eyelids at exactly five-thirty and turned his alarm clock off before it had a chance to make a noise.

He dressed and geared up for the day, and as he sat chatting quietly over a cup of Maddie's coffee, he wondered what his appointment with the good Reverend Bodean might have in store for him. The pulsing ache at the back of his head had softened by then from the ibuprofen he chewed on his way out the door. Maddie's coffee did little to diminish the bitter taste of the pills.

———◆———

"What time do you have, Annie?" Reverend Bodean asked the church secretary while peeking around her office door.

"It's not even nine o'clock and that's the third time you've asked me that question," she barked back at him. "He'll be here when he gets here."

Jimmy scurried toward his office.

Cowboy was angling his truck through town on the same route as his previous year's visit, on very nearly the same perfect fall day. The sun was bright and crisp and the shadows from the oak and maple trees stretched long across the street. He pulled into the same parking lot, where the same Chevy van was parked nose to nose with the same Lincoln Continental. He even managed to land his tire in the same deep pothole, causing a laugh to bounce out of his chest.

He looked up in time to see Reverend Bodean appear in the front double doors. He climbed the front steps of the church, and the reverend stretched out his hand to greet Cowboy. "Sorry about that pothole," he said. "We've been meaning to get that thing fixed."

"Nonsense," Cowboy insisted. "I park there on purpose. When the nose of my truck drops that far, it makes my fuel gauge read a full quarter of a tank higher. Good to see you, Reverend. You look good. How have you been?" Cowboy shook Jimmy's hand three times sharply, but the reverend did not let go immediately; he stood there behind his brilliant, broad smile, examining Cowboy.

"Good to see you!" he exclaimed. "I've been really good."

"I see the church's Christmas program has you growing that

beard again." Cowboy nodded at the snow-white growth. "There is no limit to the misery we will endure for loved ones, eh?" Cowboy smiled.

"Misery indeed," the reverend agreed. "This thing itches like poison oak for the first month. Makes me wonder why I bother shaving it off in the interim."

"Because it makes you look much older than you are. Beards are making a fashion comeback, though. You are aware of that, aren't you?"

"They have not been fashionable since before the razor was invented, which should tell you everything you need to know about beards. If they can be removed, they should be." The reverend's observation made Cowboy laugh out loud. "Come on. I'll escort you to the furnace room."

The two men took an immediate left down the stairs instead of entering the sanctuary. Across the basement floor and a jingle of a key ring later and the two were standing in a well-lit, extremely clean boiler room. The hot water storage tank was sporting a brand-new paint job and there wasn't a sign of a leak anywhere near the building. The boiler was firing, and upon looking through the new glass of the furnace peephole, Cowboy could see that the combustion ratios were set perfectly.

A better look around the room showed the old relief valve on the work bench had been disassembled, cleaned, reassembled, and tested, and was waiting to resume its duties should the new relief valve start leaking. Under the bench was a keg of water treatment chemicals, and hanging on the peg board above it Cowboy could see the results of the water testing that had been done over the previous twelve months.

"Very impressive. It's remarkable what a little time and attention can do for this equipment. Well done." Cowboy verified the settings of the new relief valve, checked the position of the gas train vents, and nodded at Reverend Bodean to let him know that he was done.

The reverend set his hand gently on Cowboy's left shoulder to guide him from the room. "C'mon," he told him. "There's something else I want to show you." Reverend Bodean pulled the light-bulb string and closed the door to the darkness as they left the furnace room and made their way across the basement to the staircase. A moment later they found themselves crossing the sanctuary and standing in front of Annie's desk, her chin pointing directly at her large breasts as she eyed them both over the top of her horn-rimmed glasses.

"Can I see the bill sheets?" Reverend Bodean asked with a wide, toothy grin.

"You already looked at them," Annie answered with a scowl.

"Yeah, yeah. I know. But I want to see them again."

Reluctantly, Annie pulled the contents out of her half empty "IN" basket on the front right corner of her old oak teacher's desk and began rifling through the short stack of pages. She pulled a colorful single-page spreadsheet titled "expenses" and handed it to Jimmy while scowling at Cowboy.

"Here." He handed the spreadsheet to Cowboy. "Take a look."

Cowboy took little notice of Annie's frown and squinted at the different colors aligned by column on the spreadsheet. This particular page showed the previous twelve months of utility expenses for the church, with the red column showing the gas bills, the blue column showing the water bills, and the green showing the electric expenses. With a quick calculation in his head, Cowboy could see that the utilities maintenance costs increased the previous November by just over six hundred dollars, but the gas bills since then had been reduced by nearly 60 percent. The water bills were down by over 40 percent and electric bills by about 20 percent. "It looks like the chemical cleaning and repairs cost you a bit, but wow!" Cowboy exclaimed. "Look at how much you saved!"

Reverend Bodean took the spreadsheet that Cowboy handed back and glanced at it before returning it to Annie. He had studied the expenses in detail and did not need to look again. The numbers were right. "It is the first time in three years that the church has met its utility budget, thanks to you." The reverend smiled brightly at Cowboy, but Annie just pursed her lips tightly as she continued looking down her nose at him.

"Thanks to me?" Cowboy blushed slightly. "I didn't do anything but recognize the opportunity. You were the ones that had to take advantage of it."

"C'mon," Reverend Bodean told him again. This time he threw his arm around both of Cowboy's shoulders to guide him from the church secretary's office. He almost had to stand on his toes to do it, but Jimmy managed to wrestle his way to the door with the taller figure beside him. "There's something else I want to show you." He dropped his arm while crossing the threshold and entering the hallway. He led Cowboy to his office three doors down the hall from Annie's.

As the two men entered Reverend Bodean's office, Cowboy nearly had to squint against the brilliance of the room. The smell of fresh paint and varnish, the shutters wide open, and the one window against the far wall on the left was opened wide to allow the smell of the rose garden planted along the back fence of the playground area to mingle with the newness of Jimmy's refurbished office. Although the office had the same furniture, the place had an entirely new personality about it. It was playful, inviting, and refreshing.

"My son and I overhauled the place this summer with a hundred-dollar bill and a lot of elbow grease. He picked the colors from one of Annie's *Country Living* magazines, and we polished and recoated these old oak floors. Looks pretty good. Don't you think?"

"It looks magnificent." Cowboy was truly impressed by the transformation. The walls had a soft green color and the shutters were painted teal. All of the rose vases were gone save for the one that held the Issey Miyake perfume resting on the corner of Jimmy's spotless desk. Everything was set squarely in its place and there wasn't a speck of dust anywhere in the room. The bookshelves were alphabetized and well-lit, and the floor had a mirror shine on it. "Absolutely magnificent," Cowboy told him again, stunned. "This is certainly not the same place you were holed up in last year." He smiled at Jimmy

"Jay-jay and I really had a lot of fun doing it. We were so delighted with the results, we immediately followed up by doing his room at home. He's excited to show his cousin his new room. My nephew is coming back early from his college break to visit for a few days."

"Is he coming back from Texas?" The wheels were turning furiously as Cowboy asked the reverend.

Jimmy had a mild look of shock on his face. "Yes," he said as he stared back at Cowboy. Cowboy held up his hand, shaking his head slightly in a "never mind" fashion. "But," Reverend Bodean added, "that's not what I wanted to show you." Jimmy slipped across the floor and sat behind his desk. "Come. Sit." He pointed at the heavily dented chair in front of his desk, then took a stack of trifold flyers from his desk, setting them in front of Cowboy next to the solved Rubik's cube. "Here," he said nodding at the stack of flyers. "Take a look."

Cowboy lifted one from the top of the stack and began reading. It was a notice that had undoubtedly been inserted in the usher's handouts when the church bells rang the call to church. Jimmy was beaming over the description of the new youth ministry that had started just eight weeks ago. The flyer described all the people volunteering, the activities being undertaken, transportation offered, and scheduled speakers, with credits offered along the back panel of all the people donating to the endeavor. The front panel had a recent photograph of Jimmy and his son captioned as *Reverend Bodean and Jim Junior start a new youth ministry*.

"This is what we have been doing with all the extra money we saved from getting the heating systems in order." Reverend Bodean looked like he was about to start passing out cigars.

"This is great stuff. I bet the kids are so excited. I see you kicked this thing off just a few months ago. Unbelievable! Really good stuff you've got here. Cowboy sounded as if he were getting ready to pass out cigars. "How's it going so far?" Cowboy inquired, tilting his head slightly.

"It's early yet, but the program is off to a great start." Jimmy sounded positive and upbeat, but hesitant. "The response to the new program has been great by the kids in town, but it did not really incite the response I was hoping to get."

Leaning in slightly, Cowboy asked, "And what was the response you were hoping to get?"

"Well, we were hoping that getting the kids in the community involved in this program would motivate their parents into attending regular services again, but attendance at the regular services has stayed remarkably flat. Did you know that only about twenty percent of Christians actually attend church regularly?" Reverend Bodean's brow furrowed slightly, but he somehow remained smiling at Cowboy.

"I didn't realize it was so low. With Christians numbering about seventy-five percent of the country's population, that would mean a small town of say, ten thousand people, about seventy-five hundred would actually claim to be Christian, and only about fifteen hundred of them attend church regularly. It doesn't seem like much, does it? How many do you have in your congregation?" Cowboy asked.

"We have a hundred and seventeen, but only about sixty attend church regularly."

"I'd take a guess that about half are kids under the age of twelve and the other half consists largely of their parents. So, let's say twenty-five percent, or fifteen of them are men. I'd take another guess that about half of them have bruises where their wives prod them with sticks to motivate them into attending and keep them awake during services. That sound about right?"

"Yeah." Jimmy agreed, not really surprised that Cowboy knew the statistics and expressed them so generally. The reverend chuckled at the thought of some of his women parishioners poking their husbands with sticks.

"Did you know that only about seventeen percent of children continue coming to church after reaching adulthood if their mother is the only parent bringing them? That percentage goes up to forty-one if the father is the only one bringing them while they are growing up, and it goes up to seventy-two percent if both parents are herding their children to church."

"Really?" Reverend Bodean pondered the information. "Why do you suppose that is?"

"Some would say it is because mothers are busy raising children, while fathers are busy raising adults. Othes might put it more simply by saying that women are crazy."

Both men laughed. "I'm not sure what that means," Jimmy admitted.

"From the beginning of time, whether by genetics or culture, women are very typically non-linear in their thought processes. They've historically been tasked with budgeting the family funds, raising the children, cooking dinners, providing medical attention, working, church, laundry, and whatever else was needed, whereas the men were tasked with earning money or hunting, or fixing what broke. Women are multi-talented multitaskers. Men have a tendency to focus on the task at hand. To put it another way, when a linear-thinking man wants to get from point A to point C, he simply travels through B. On the other hand, when a woman wants to get from point A to point C, she may beat the alphabet to death to get there. She wants to call W and see if they would like to come along, and be certain U is not offended, since they don't much care for C. You get the picture," Cowboy explained.

"I'm not sure I follow."

"A woman's belief in God and her tendency to attend church may only make sense to her. As such, the grown children may not continue because they can't follow her elevated train of thought. A father, on the other hand, has a much simpler thought process, so if he's going to church, it must make sense, if only to him. Those men napping here Sunday mornings may not know why they believe in God, or are even sure that they do believe in God, but they do know that wherever they lead, their family will follow. They also know there are a lot worse places to lead a family. The bottom line is that women aren't crazy. They are simply so much smarter and so much more complex than we are." Cowboy reached for his hat twice and realized he hadn't worn it due to the tenderness of his knotted head. He stood to make his way toward the exit and was overcome with vertigo again. Reverend Bodean asked if he was okay, watching him swoon against the front of his desk.

"I'm good." Cowboy softened at the look of concern on the reverend's face. "Rapped myself on the noodle the other day and it's still a bit tender is all."

"I'm still not sure I'm following your tracks here," the reverend stated as he stood. "What's this got to do with our new children's ministry?"

As they strolled toward the front of the church, Cowboy noticed the piercing glance thrown by Annie as they passed her office doorway. "It's pretty simple," Cowboy explained. "If you want to grow the church, you simply need to get the men in the community to attend, instead of focusing on the children."

"And how would I go about that?" Jimmy asked under a muffled guffaw.

"Back during World War Two, Roy Rogers once told Winston Churchill that he knew how to keep the Germans from invading England. He told him that he simply needed to set the Atlantic Ocean on fire. When Churchill asked him how he was to go about that, Rogers told him he didn't know, he was simply the idea man." Cowboy smiled at Reverend Bodean. "I don't know how you get the men in your community to attend church. Men are pretty simple and very linear in their thought processes. I would think the best place to start is to prove God exists. Once they know that, they'll come flocking, dragging their families behind."

"Yeah, right!" Jimmy's voice was escalating slightly with frustration. "How on earth am I supposed to prove God's existence?"

Cowboy shoved the heavy double doors of the church front open and embraced the warm brilliance of the morning sun with his eyes closed. "The question is not if you believe in God, Reverend." Cowboy smiled back at the sun with his eyes still closed. "The question is why do you believe in God."

"Well...I just know He's real," Reverend Bodean offered in a stammering, unsure way. "When I was a boy...there was this thing that happened..."

Cowboy held up his left hand waist high. "I know you believe. The question of why often comes with some experience we've encountered that is usually all too easily explained by the science we've earned through the tree of knowledge. I want you to prove God exists." Cowboy still had his eyes closed facing the sun on the top step at the church's front doors. He blinked them open and looked directly at the reverend. "Women aren't crazy. They've just got nothing to prove." He smiled broadly.

Jimmy looked up, smiling back. "So why do you believe?"

"You seem to be a fan of statistics. Let me offer you a few." Cowboy went back to softly gazing at the trees on the horizon, listening peacefully to the gentle gust rustling the grounded leaves. "Did you know that seventy-four percent of children raised by an alcoholic parent become alcoholics themselves? Sixty-one percent of those raised by a drug addict become addicts as well." Cowboy's gaze and voice softened as he continued. "Thirty-three percent of abused children become abusers to their own, and thirty-five percent of kids raised by a pedophile become one as an adult."

The reverend's face sagged in a sorrowful frown. "I'll leave it to you to discern whatever goes unsaid, since it will remain that way," Cowboy finished, "but by my math, I had a total of a two hundred and three percent chance of failure. The likelihood of falling into any of it was assured more than twice over. You see, the miracle of God begins in the impossibilities."

The reverend began clutching his chest tightly and whispered, "It isn't possible for you to know my nephew is coming from Texas, at least, not possible for me to understand how you know."

"I bet young Jason is even attending Creighton University," Cowboy began, but the vertigo caused by stepping off the first concrete step overwhelmed him. He lurched for the handrail and didn't even come close to catching it with his flailing hand. Down he tumbled with the awestruck reverend chasing quickly behind.

9

BACK TO THE VERY BEGINNING

I.

At exactly 3:53 AM, I was gently guided out of sleep and into a state of full alertness. I was in bed again, but alone. I was not exactly in bed, but above it. Levitating peacefully, I couldn't identify my surroundings at first, but as I spun around, afloat on my axis, I could see a priest in the room next to me, and whatever was left of me lying on the bed directly below.

"The priest was right, you know?" I could feel the voice whispering in my tailbone and slowly creeping up my tingling spine. I spun back to face the tiled ceiling. It felt strange to move without friction or gravity to push against. His face was inverted. He was holding me in His lap, looking down into my eyes.

"Right about what?" I asked.

"That it really is a simple matter of perspective," He said, lifting me gently to a sitting position. "Come on, it's time for a field trip."

I was saddened at sitting upright. I wanted to stay right there, pulsing and vibrating with my head resting on His thigh. I wanted to stay right there and soak in the blissful, Superman, fearful, excited feeling with His fingers running gently through my hair. We both stood and I looked back at whatever that was of me lying in the bed below, with tubes and wires and the darkness of a deathly aura encircling it...me. "But what about...?" I was pointing back at the lifeless figure on the bed, lying flat on its back with undisturbed, sterile covers pressed just up to its chest.

"Don't worry about that," God answered. "I've much to show you. Come on." He encouraged again behind a smile that dimmed the sun. "It's field trip day!" Then He cocked His head slightly to the right, as if listening.

When I glanced over at the priest, he was barely breathing, lying on his left side and curled in the fetal position. Every breath was labored and followed by a soft moan. The scar on his right cheek looked deeper, whiter, and more pronounced. "Don't worry about him either," God said, nudging me from behind now. "We'll take care of that when we get back."

We? was all I could think before we burst from the room, the hospital, the city lights, elevating and accelerating away from the earth and past the moon, away from the sun and out to where we had a full view of the Milky Way before stopping to gather in the sight. The sensation of immediate distance and the overpowering silence of watching the galaxy's methodical, slow spinning left me breathless. *An accurate description*, I thought through the fear. *Breathless in space.* The terror immediately subsided when I caught hold of one loose end of the braided cincture holding His robes loosely against His waist.

"Hang on!" He laughed like a father on a carnival ride. "We're not even close yet!" He held His index finger straight up to the height of His chest and rapidly spun it counterclockwise as the swirl of starlight began to spin wildly.

"Close to what?" I screamed against flashing lights of even further instantaneous distance and tightening my grasp around the wrist-sized rope.

"To the beginning!" He laughed His loud, open laugh. Everything—literally everything—was suddenly spinning backward and collapsing, and He reached out both arms to embrace it all as it shrunk into a mass that He could reach around. It kept growing smaller and smaller, and then it divided into two distinctly different orbs, with one glowing blackly in His outstretched right hand, and the other radiating white hot in the left hand.

Nothing but the blackness of an eternal void surrounded us. "I don't understand," I stuttered, tightening my grip on the cincture even more. "Did everything just shrink? Or did we just grow?" I reached over and held on with both hands now. Even though the sensation of movement was gone, the feeling of unrestricted floating and now nothing to stand on remained.

"You see," He said, smiling down at me and passing the white orb to join the other, holding them both in His right hand and spinning them around His palm like a pair of Chinese Shouxing balls. "That's what I like about you." He looked at me, tapping me gently on the right cheek in a familiar way. "Perspective." He smiled even broader. He cocked Head again, as if listening to some intangible, distant noise.

"In this case," He continued, "perspective is much less relevant." He separated the balls again into each of His hands and started contact juggling them in opposing directions, rolling them around His hands and up His arms without ever losing touch with them. "Substance, time, size, distance...all of it doesn't matter much here."

"Wh-where?" I asked.

"Here with Me. There's only Me and the life of Me. See?" He faced me, threw the black orb up into nothing, and swiped His right hand through me. Like smoke, whatever it was that I was made up of briefly followed His hand before collecting back to where it started in my midsection. He laughed again and caught the falling orb in His open palm. "It may take Me a few minutes. Well, actually, if you read about it, it took Me a few days, but I've been putting these two together." He studied the two balls closely and began pressing them together at chest level.

I was perplexed at the way He spoke in present tense and past tense when referencing the same thing. "You were, or You are?" I asked.

"Yes," He said with a chuckle. "Haven't you heard? I am that I am. I am the butcher and the baker, the policeman and the criminal, the housewife, the lawyer, the engineer, and the gardener. Before you can delve into what I am, or why I am, you must first accept *that* I am." He lifted His right ear again. "Yes. Yes. I know. Just a minute," He answered no one.

He then placed His hands together and held them tightly between His thighs for leverage. I focused all of my attention on the two orbs in His hands and they appeared to meld and consume each other. "Matter and antimatter, or the light and the darkness, or the yin and yang, the beginning and end, or life and death. Whatever you prefer to call it." His muscles were taut, forcing the two together. "You see, there cannot be one without the other, and both are needed for this."

I stared at the orbs coming together in the perfect symbol of Chinese philosophy, each orb trying to overtake the other, growing and swimming into each other, swelling and glowing over one side, only to diminish on the other, becoming one orb. "Almost there," He said, pushing the two together even harder as I moved in for a closer look. I could see through His hands, could see through the mixture melding and solidifying, and the burst that overtook us terrified me. The explosion of rays of colored light and material flying through us in a single enormous exploding sphere, spinning and swirling, twisting and collecting across the blackness of the void; a magnificent firework tearing through the darkness in all directions away from us where He was the center. "There!" He announced, shaking His hands like they were stinging. "That was harder than I remember." He laughed still talking in past and present tense.

With enough courage finally building in me, I let go with one hand and pointed at moving colors slowly twirling into substance. "It's magnificent." I was dumbfounded.

"Well, it's okay. Give me a second." He raised His index finger again and twirled it in a clockwise direction. Everything began spinning faster, coalescing and congealing, as we flew around the perimeter watching with Him still twirling His finger into space and raising His left arm in front of us. We drifted slowly toward the interior of the sphere and stopped right where we began, in full view of the slow-spinning, newly formed Milky Way.

We're back at the beginning again, I thought.

"I always find it interesting how so many are working toward the end, when the truth is every moment is a new beginning. Now watch this," He said with a sly smile. He stood and seemed to grow, watching the drifting meteors of the Kuiper Belt pass in front of Him like a lazy river of flowing rock. He would pick one up, roll it around in His hands, and put it back into the flow. "There's a good one!" He looked like a young boy picking skipping stones. He rubbed His hands over the stone, wearing it into a perfect ball. I could see the smoky mist of Himself collecting all over the surface of the rock as He rolled it and rubbed it and blew on it.

Then He stood with His left foot in front of His right, with His arms swinging low at each side, winding up. He even nodded politely at a catcher who wasn't there before lifting His arms over his head and stretching forward. His colors were pulsing and mingling and His appearance altered to the slightest, recognizable faces. He vaulted forward with the stretch and appearance of Randy Johnson, somehow altering into the unmistakable, left-handed power of Nolan Ryan, and finishing with the baffling sidearm of a Satchel Paige curveball, and sent the rock blazing toward the hot iron ball that was once, or is now, earth. His smoky light particles trailing off and the speed of the meteor made it look like a huge tracer bullet when it smashed directly into the spinning mass of earth, hitting it so hard, it knocked the moon out to orbit the reshaping and now glowing globe.

The ensuing explosion shook the entire solar system. "Strike!" He yelled triumphantly.

"What was that?" I yelled back at Him.

"That, young man, was some of me spreading over all of that," He explained, pointing at the settling earth. "Now, want to see something truly magnificent?" He raised His index finger again and began spinning it slower now in the well-lit universe. I floated and watched as time flashed through a million years a second. The zinc and carbon and oxygen and hydrogen and iron collated and collected, growing and changing and evolving at Godspeed.

Small cellular combinations grew into barely mobile predators, which grew into massive oceanic predators feeding on those that swam through the seaweed growing across the expanse of the seas. I was mesmerized, and when I spun to ask where these miracles went, I saw Him crouched down on His kneecaps, rolling a much smaller meteor in His fingers and shoving it toward His crooked thumb and second knuckle of His index finger. Snapping His thumb forward, the meteor was sent racing toward the inhabited world.

The marble smashed into the earth, causing a dark cloud of dust around the entire top half. Ice was melting and rivers were flowing, and as the dust settled, the tectonic plates shifted, forcing land masses to rise out of the oceans. The creatures began migrating out of the water and onto land, growing legs, chasing others through the newly formed trees and plant life.

"I got your steely!" He yelped, tauntingly. "One more shot wins the game." He was laughing and polishing the end of His cue stick with chalk, His colors flashing and pulsing. He polished another meteor from those flowing by, lined it up, and punched it solidly with the cue stick, driving it into the dead center of the earth. Another cloud of dust and ash plumed off the surface, settling again to the blue orb swarming with life.

"Here it comes." He beamed at His work. "Now take a look," He ordered as He collected Himself into His original appearance. He threw His right arm around my shoulders and cast out His left, drawing us closer and closer to the world at the time. We hovered above the collected continents that were once Africa and watched as a new animal emerged, upright, and bipedal. "There they are," He announced, looking ready to start passing out cigars. "Watch him study. Watch him learn. He migrates out and back, but always comes back to this single spot and sits near that tree." God Himself looked a bit mesmerized.

The creature was dirty and hairy and appeared contemplative. As the moons rose and fell, he would fast forward out during the days and back to that same spot during the nights, watching the moon rise and fall at different phases and different positions on the horizon and standing guard over his family while the fruit of the tree would bud, ripen, and reseed the ground around it. He was correlating the position of the moon to the seasons, and the seasons to the ripening fruit that he counted as a staple food. God's index finger continued to spin slowly as I watched the stakes driven, the temples built, the forested ground churned and plowed, and tribes and villages morphing into cities; wars being waged and machines for conquering constructed; borders and battle lines drawn and redrawn.

"Why couldn't they stay where they were?" I asked.

"Hey, I tried to warn them."

"Yes, but You gave them a choice knowing what they would choose," I said with some indignation. "You knew they would choose to eat from that tree. To watch and study and farm and outgrow themselves."

"They had to." He looked quiet and watchful. Then He turned His head and looked directly at me. "Love that is not chosen is not unconditional, and I wanted them to learn how to love unconditionally." His eyes were softer now behind an understanding smile. We were sitting in a reclined position on nothing, as if at a theater playing a must-see movie.

"You wanted them to have the opportunity to love as You do." I nodded in understanding.

"Now you're catching on, My boy." He reached over to slap me on the shoulder, and before His hand could pass unimpeded through it, He stopped it short on my back for effect. "Loving this one you call Adam was easy when he could do no wrong. He needed to know that I loved him no matter what wrong he did. It's a good thing I created him a helper, or else nothing would have gotten done." He smiled. "But, you failed to grasp the essence of the field trip."

"And what was that?" I couldn't believe there was more to it, but He smiled deeply at me.

"I keep an infinite watch over this finite element of life I placed here," He said, pointing at the earth without taking His gaze off me. "You have seen here that, in order for you to live, something else must die."

"That's true for every living thing down there," I said, nodding at earth.

"Yes. You see. Everything is symbiotic. The grass nourishes the gazelle, and the gazelle nourishes the cheetah, and when the cheetah dies, he nourishes the grass."

"You lost me."

"Over the last twelve billion years, some part of you has been a part of every living thing on that planet. It has taken Me that long to plan and collect the exact molecular components that you are made up of, and a manipulation of the circumstances you've experienced over your brief life since the time you were born to develop your single perspective. No one on earth looks or thinks or acts or feels exactly as you do."

I smiled at the thought.

"It has taken Me twelve billion years to create you, and there has never, ever been another one of you before." He offered a lengthy pause. "And if I keep this world going for another twelve billion years, there will never be another one of you." He looked deeply at me, almost pleadingly. "Do you see how special you are to Me?"

"Yes," I answered. "I believe I do."

He slipped behind me and draped His arm over my shoulder so He could pull me closer and whisper directly into my ear. "Now do you see how special they all are to Me, each and every one, a custom design of Mine to shine the briefest, brightest light?"

"Yes," I repeated. "I believe I do."

"And now, do you see how special you are to them?"

"Can I go back now?"

"But My son, I thought you wanted to stay here with Me. It's all you've ever wanted." He smiled at the student learning the lesson well.

"I know, but now I know."

"Know what?" He asked, knowing perfectly well what it was I knew.

"I know that to serve them is to serve You...even if they don't want me to."

"Yes." He slid around in front of me to look directly at me. "Especially if they don't want you to. Remember. He washed their feet and told them to love their enemies, because now they can choose to do so. Now, there is the small matter of our agreement."

"Our agreement?" I whined. "How could I possibly leave You something when there is nothing of me here?" I flayed my hands through myself, stirring up the smoky mist I consisted of.

"But there is something I need to make your next project achievable." He was patient and terribly kind about my exasperation.

"What is that?"

"I need you," He answered with a smile.

I was puzzled. "I don't understand."

"I need you to give Me all of you."

"But I'm not holding on to anything. I don't have any tobacco or swearing tendencies. I don't even have any pants!" I exclaimed, looking through my open palms at the rest of me. "How can I give you what I don't have?" I felt His patience and kept my hands in front of me.

"All of your anguish and mistrust; all of your cynicism and unforgiveness and anger." His expression saddened. He knew the effort that would be required to complete the task. He knew exactly how much suffering and pain had accumulated in His traveling companion through the course of his life, and He knew how desperately I clung to that pain, watching it constantly and gripping it tightly to ensure it never had the chance of getting loose or happening to me again. "You've held on to these things long enough and you've no more need for them. They will only serve to hinder you on this next project." His compassion overflowed.

"But, isn't...doesn't..."

"No," He interrupted softly. "These things don't make you witty or charming, and they certainly do not make you unique. I understand them, but they serve you no good purpose. If you want to be unique, give these things to Me."

I began to weep deeply.

"Look again," He insisted.

I looked down at the misty fog of myself; at my hands and arms; at my lower extremities. I could even see my own reflection on the surface of Him. More accurately, I could see through myself. I could see the darkened areas of the scars above each eye, along each arm, and across my back and legs from a childhood riddled with beatings. I could see the black splotches of the drugs and alcohol and sex used to hide the pain. "What is this?" I asked through a sob that came from so deep inside it felt as though I were vomiting around a closed throat.

"These were your responses to the circumstances I created for exactly the right perspective of you, but they are no longer needed. You were right, you know." He smiled briefly through the gravity of the situation.

"Right about what?" I managed to ask through the lifetime of sorrow welling up within me.

"These are not things you have to give up. You simply have to give them back." A tear of compassion began to well in His eyes.

"But there will be nothing left of me." I was panting heavily, trying to control the uncontrollable sadness falling over me. My hands were over my face and I fell to my knees onto nothing, wailing under the weight.

"Yes." He reached down and began running His fingers through my hair. "I know, but these defenses you have built only serve to get in the way. Come to Me and I will defend you." He pulled me to my feet and held His arms open as an invitation. "Come to me, My son, and take Me to the world through the perspective I have given you."

I stepped forward with my arms out, walking into His endless embrace. A warm peacefulness surrounded me as I passed through Him, swirling across Him, engulfing myself within Him. At coming through Him, the immense Superman feeling overcame me, twice as acute as any time before. When I looked down at myself again, the darkened stains and splotches had vanished. We both turned to face each other and I could see all of the misery of my life had been purged from me and remained with Him, popping like tiny balloons as they lingered momentarily, only to be consumed by His light.

He didn't even wince at the lifetime of the pain I left behind. Through His widening smile, He took my face in both hands. "You belong to Me. You know that, don't you?"

"Yes," I answered Him directly with my sorrow so far gone.

He took one hand from my cheek and opened it in front of us. "And all of this," He continued showing me the universe, "every part of Me belongs to you."

We fell straight down while He stood there facing me and holding my shoulders now. Down into North America; down into the center of the United States; down into the city and the hospital room, and we were instantly back above the hospital bed, back to where we began, where the rest of me lay. We were hovering face-to-face, with mine toward the ceiling and His almost touching mine. Nurse Morgan was deeply sobbing in the corner of the room darkened by the moonless night. "You really want to go back?" He asked.

"Yes, but I don't know...I can't figure out how..." I was fumbling my search for words.

"Well then," He said, grinning, "all you need is a little push in the right direction." I could hear an annoying blipping sound in the background...blip...blip...blip. He shoved hard at my shoulders He held in His hands. In my shock, I dropped instantly back on the bed and inside that part of me that still lay there with the blip getting more insistent...BLIP...BLIP...BLIP. In the moment I descended, I heard Him say, "If you really want Me to hear your prayers, make sure you're praying for someone else, and tell the priest I said hello to his grandson."

10

THE RESURRECTION

I.

BLIP...BLIP...BLIP. He fluttered his eyes and focused on the soundproofing holes in the ceiling tile. The EKG blipped softly near his head as he collected his senses, lying very still. Nurse Morgan covered the scream threatening to escape her mouth with both hands as she approached his bedside, looking down at him. Tears were still streaming down her shocked expression.

"You were..." she paused. "You died!" The seriousness of her training took over and she immediately reached for the call button.

"Don't," He told her. "Don't call anyone yet. Just give me a minute, please."

She could see the pleading in his eyes and hesitated. Every joint and muscle in his body bellowed with movement, but Cowboy raised his hand and took the one she had reached to call for help. "Please," he begged. "Just one minute." He tried to sit upright, but the pure white hot iron in his bones required Morgan to help.

"I really need to call the ER doctor." She hesitated again as he swung his legs out of the bed, moaning against the pain. She knew doing anything else could be at the expense of her job.

"Yes, you do." Cowboy groaned at the pain of standing. "Just not yet." He baby-stepped across the space between his bed and

Father Billings while leaning softly on Nurse Morgan walking slowly beside him. As he approached the half-raised rail on the side of the priest's bed, he studied him. His eyes were open, but Father Billings was not seeing anything through the glaze formed over them. Every breath was a battle for him as his lungs rattled, and he was little more than a pile of bones.

"I told him when you arrived in the emergency room. The swelling in your brain...you were in pretty bad shape. He insisted you be put in here with him. That was when he was still talking."

"How long?" Cowboy asked.

"That was four days ago. The day after you handed me this." She slid a small business card out of the front pocket of her smock and showed it to him. "That's also when he stopped eating."

"He stopped eating and talking because he threw himself into prayer and fasting."

"Praying for what?" she asked.

"For me." He took the priest's right hand dangling through the bed rail. He bowed his head slightly, lifted his eyes to the universe, and whispered, "Well, here *we* are." Cowboy listened and looked around the sterile room, waiting for something...*anything.*

When he looked back down at the priest, he suddenly saw a darkness overtaking his body. It was not as though Cowboy could see through him, but more like he could see into the priest, and the deathly shadows were drowning out the smaller white flashes of light. The priest's hand tightened furiously around Cowboy's and he saw the blackness within the priest start to migrate. Cowboy clasped the back of Chuck's grip with his free hand and watched the darkness collect and flow from his chest and abdomen, creeping up his shoulders and down his arm toward their clenched hands. He leaned over and whispered directly into the priest's exposed ear. "You let him go now. I need him." It wasn't a command he issued, but a soft, insistent request.

Father Billings was shuddering and sweating as the darkness flowed out of him and through Cowboy's hands reaching his elbow before dissipating into the small desk lamp on his nightstand.

Morgan's eyes had dried in a widening stare. Although her mouth had fallen open, there were no words to tumble out of her shaking chin. Father Billings ignored the tubes hanging from his left arm as he wrapped it around Cowboy's shoulders drawing him closer. "It's about damn time, you wild man," he whispered in his raspy growl. "Where the hell have you been?" He smiled broadly as Cowboy helped him to a seated position on the bed.

"I've been a little busy," He told him, smiling back, and then advised. "You're gonna want to keep that swearing in check or there could be a painful lesson in it for you." Cowboy laughed quietly.

"I'm starving," Chuck announced, looking directly at the nurse, who was still frozen in astonishment. "Any chance a guy could get a sandwich around here?" He swung his legs over the side of his bed and tentatively reached his dangling toes toward the floor.

Morgan bounced straight up on her toes at the shock of hearing the priest's voice. All she could muster at that moment was "Uh…"

The priest gently laid his hand on her forearms, which were tightly clenched against her breasts. "It's okay, sweetie." She was still debating whether to push the call button or run to the cafeteria. "You have some choices here." He spoke to her softly. "You could call in the National Guard, who would insist on studying us for weeks on end, or you could tell no one what has happened here, since none of us are quite sure how to explain it anyway." His soft eyes were fixed directly on hers. The scar down the side of his cheek was faded now, and his eyes became clear and crisp with focus.

"I'll be right back," she told us, as her soft white leather shoes padded quickly toward the door. "Don't go anywhere." We watched her close the door quietly behind her as she left the room.

"Now what?" Father Billings ripped the tape and pulled the tubes from his arm.

"I have no idea."

"Well, we can't stay here." He stood shakily in his white hospital pajama bottoms and stumbled toward the closet. Cowboy was naked under an open-back hospital gown. "They took all your IV tubes and the shunt in your head out when you died over there," he informed, nodding once at the empty bed across the room. He handed over a small sack containing Cowboy's wallet, watch, cell phone and belt. "They also cut all your clothes off examining you in the emergency room." He seemed to find great humor in Cowboy's nudity.

"But Morgan said she'd be coming back."

"Yeah. Since when do I listen to a nurse?" The priest chuckled quietly. "Here," he said, poking a pair of his pants at Cowboy that he'd removed from the closet shelf as he donned the full-length black trench coat hanging from the rod.

"I wasn't really dead." Cowboy was trying desperately to believe his own words.

"I've been told that nothing ever really dies." Cowboy found little comfort in Chuck's explanation, remembering that, in order for anything to live, something else must die. "Whatever you call it, I've seen enough of it in my life to recognize it. Yeah," he said, watching Cowboy slip the borrowed pants up to his waist and fasten them. They were too short for his legs but fit at the midriff. "You were dead." He said it so knowingly that Cowboy had no choice but to believe him.

They took an immediate right out of the room down a polished, dimly lit corridor and through the double doors marked *Staff Only.* It looked to be the middle of the night, and the hallway was quiet and empty as they walked toward the elevator with the same restriction of *Staff Only* posted above the floor buttons. Cowboy punched the lighted button on for the lobby, knowing there would be no one staffing the front information desk, and the two walked out the front doors of the hospital.

They made it the two blocks to a fast-food restaurant before stepping in for warmth. Their feet were cold with nothing on but hospital slippers, and the teenager behind the counter eyed them suspiciously until Cowboy ordered two super-sized value meals with coffee and used his Uber app to get a ride. The driver called asking if they really needed an Uber cab for ninety miles. The location was confirmed and the driver was promised a healthy tip after he agreed to the terms. He let them know he would arrive shortly.

Cowboy figured his place was their best bet under the current circumstances. He had a minor mess to clean up; first with Mike and then with Christy. He looked at his cell and noted thirty-four missed phone calls, most of which were from those two, not only because of the missed plane heading to Abu Dhabi, but because they both genuinely cared.

They finished their meals quickly, still grappling with what they had been through, and stepped back in the cold air to wait the last five minutes for the cab. The priest carried the last handful of his fries with him. "How is that poor nurse going to explain our disappearance?" Cowboy asked with mild worry.

"She won't, and neither will any of the hospital staff," the priest answered. "The administrator will simply state that we discharged ourselves and left. How else do you explain the two of us leaving your hospital?"

"I guess there's no sense in worrying. We were both dead ten minutes ago." Cowboy smiled at the thought of getting a do-over; the thought of being born again.

"Now what?" the priest asked, munching on the remains of his heavily salted fries.

"I have no idea." Cowboy was honest and direct. "I was hoping you could tell me. I'm not sure what to do, other than love the world. They're going to love us."

"That's where you're only half right. The other half will despise us. You see...perspective."

As if puffing dust from a windowsill, a gust of wind swirled a stirring of leaves around their feet, raising the priest's black trench coat and Cowboy's white hospital gown, circling them into a perfect overhead view of the yin and yang.

"There is one thing though."

Chuck poked the last three fries into his mouth and pressed his hand directly on Cowboy's shoulder. "What's that?" he mumbled around the fries.

"I've been asked to inquire about your grandson." Cowboy

didn't know what he was talking about, but the gape that crossed the priest's face said that he surely knew.

"Ja...I always thought...but how?" His stunned expression was defining and the only words that came to his mouth as the Uber driver pulled up, eyeing them suspiciously, were "Son of a bi... OOOWWWW!"

"I warned you about that swearing," Cowboy chuckled as they climbed into the car. "How's that salt feel on that fresh bite to your tongue?" he added, breaking into a full laugh.

EPILOGUE: COMING TOGETHER

They arrived at the house and paid the concerned Uber driver, tipping even more heavily than promised. Father Billings wept for the first half hour of the ninety-mile drive, and through this time, Cowboy learned that he had taken a furlough with one of his squad leaders back to Houston during his tour of duty in Vietnam. He had an affair with Sergeant Mendez's sister, Julia, which resulted in the birth of a baby girl.

The priest, or Marine officer at the time, and Sergeant Mendez returned to duty in-country. Mendez's sister, Julia, later married a Texas oil man by the name of Bodean, and with the classic American family established through unwed mothers, stepfathers, half-brothers, and the like, the baby girl grew to become somewhat of a wild child. By the time she was nineteen, she was also an unwed mother to Jason, the young seminarian.

The company that Bodean worked for wanted to expand their operation, and moved the family to develop the western oil fields of Nebraska when Jimmy was a small boy. When Jimmy's older half-sister became pregnant, she was sent back to Texas to live with her grandparents. It was just how those things were handled back then. It was hard on the young woman, but through the help of her half-brother, she found sanctuary at the church. She raised the boy alone and never married. Although Father Billings never returned to Texas, he kept a distant watchful eye on his daughter and grandson, getting the boy scholarships to Creighton, and paying for all other expenses that were not covered by the university.

He told Cowboy that he could not face Sergeant Mendez's family again, after getting him killed in the war. The closest he came was escorting the body home, but he never stepped off the plane at Houston's Hobby airport. His battles were over after suffering grievous injuries trying to pull Mendez out of the fray.

Cowboy showered first and put on fresh clothes, offering Chuck a bundle of clothes and guiding him to the guest bathroom to do the same. They couldn't wash the smell of the hospital off fast enough. While Chuck showered, Cowboy answered emails.

Christy didn't respond, as it was 3:00 in the morning, but Mike was extremely relieved to hear from him. He explained the circumstances and joked that he did not believe there was any more brain damage than what he started with. Mike responded immediately, being in Abu Dhabi and right in the middle of the workday there. He said there was no problem covering at work and ordered Cowboy to take whatever time was needed to get better. Cowboy abstained from telling Mike he'd never felt better in his life.

Father Billings appeared from the guest bathroom shirtless and refreshed, holding the borrowed T-shirt in front of him. Cowboy sadly noticed two entry wounds staggered on the right side of the priest's chest, and a large, deeply scarred exit wound from a third bullet on the left side. *Got hit coming and going*, he thought through visions of jungle battle.

"Have you got anything better than this?" he asked sincerely. "I haven't been out of uniform, whether a priest's or a Marine's, in forty years. I feel like I'm running around in my underwear with this thing on."

"Of course." Cowboy fetched him a long-sleeve white button-up to go over the tee. "You've lost so much weight through the treatments and fasting, I wasn't sure you could fill one of these out."

"How did you know I was fasting? For that matter, how did you know about Jason being my grandson?"

"It's hard to explain. The people we meet and the paths we

travel, no matter how small and insignificant they might appear, are all of immense importance if we take the time to recognize them. They are all critically connected somehow, if even in the slightest ways. It is the reason the path is so narrow. It does not lend itself to carrying anything. Those things and people we encounter on the path have not been collected by us, but been left for us to find along the way. I've even met your daughter's half-brother," Cowboy added.

"But how?" The priest looked puzzled as the implications started twirling in his mind.

"By traveling the path that has been set before me. By continuing to knock on the doors and asking the questions."

The priest finished buttoning the borrowed shirt and puzzled. "You're different...not softer, but sharper...honed somehow."

"I've been forced out of hiding." Cowboy saw the suspicious expression on Chuck's face. "Hiding from God," he finished. "We are all hiding. Hiding in our circumstances, behind our educations, in our pride, in a medicine capsule, or the bottom of a bottle. We're hiding in our anger, our diagnosis, the just causes we war over, envy, lust, our greed and even our politics. We've been hiding since we first donned fig leaves in Eden, and we've created justifications for it every step of the way."

"Where were you hiding?" Chuck's small smile faded before asking, "Where was I hiding?"

"I've been hiding in my upbringing. Packing it all silently under a cowboy hat. You? Well, you've been hiding in the past, right behind a stiff white collar." Cowboy nodded toward his desk. The first volume of Chuck's writings was still lying open in front of the stack previously collected from the bank.

The priest opened his mouth and quickly closed it upon recognizing the eleven leather binders. He walked over to the open pages and began slowly leafing through them. "I've been doing God's work." His voice wavered. "I've been seeking absolution from this..."

"No." The interruption made the priest tense his back and

shoulders. "You've been hiding in a religion that you hope will one day set you free of that past. Religion does not set us free." A tear dropped off the priest's cheek and landed on the open pages of his past. Cowboy felt the pangs of Chuck's sorrow and placed a consoling hand on his shoulder. "Religion allows a man to open his heart and let God in. Spirituality allows a man to open his heart and let God out. Which have you been doing?"

"Trying to let God in." Chuck caught a running tear with his thumb before this one fell.

"God dwells within. You cannot invite Him into His own temple." Cowboy let his hand slide off Chuck's shoulder. "And you cannot hide from the creator of all things."

"These were to help Jason...my grandson." Chuck looked up at Cowboy with reddened eyes.

"Will they help him, or are you hoping that by reading them, he will somehow help you?" Cowboy suddenly embraced the priest in understanding. "Your motivation was selfish." He held Chuck at arm's length. "Exposing that young man to these horrors will not help him."

Cowboy was pointing his open hand toward the binders. Then he closed it into a stone fist and tightly clenched his teeth. "Burn every one of them and every memory you have of this war with them." He strolled through the living room and exited the kitchen to the four-season porch and squatted in front of the large cobblestone fireplace in the corner. Lighting the tinder under the teepee of pitch wood stacked neatly on the grate brought a growing flicker of light to the room. Chuck stood frozen to the office floor watching him.

When he returned, he gathered all eleven volumes of Chuck's memoirs and carried them to the coffee table in front of the fireplace, where he spread them across its entire length like fanned playing cards. He set a heavy oak log on top of the growing blaze of pitch wood and dropped into the heavily padded rocker waiting for the priest to join him.

Within a few minutes, Chuck entered the porch and slid into the swinging loveseat resting his eyes on his contemplative friend, watching him methodically rub his whiskered chin. Cowboy sat staring into the flames and suddenly spoke without breaking his gaze. "Horse walks into a bar and orders a drink. Bartender hands him the drinks and asks, 'why the long face?'

At first, Chuck just sat there blankly staring at Cowboy. Cowboy knew it would only take the slightest nudge. Then Chuck's hinting smile grew into a grin; a grin bubbled into a chuckle, and his chuckling erupted into full guffawing laughter. "That has got to be the dumbest joke I've ever heard in my life!" The priest leaned over and grabbed a hefty volume from the fanned-out stack and pitched it on the roaring blaze. Laughter continued rolling out of him without mercy when he saw the shameless grin smear across Cowboy's face.

Cowboy realized it was the first time he had heard the priest laugh out loud. It seemed the old man's laughter dam had ruptured after decades of keeping it all acceptably contained within an endless reservoir. The relief of bursting so many pressured years flooded over them as they sat telling each other jokes. They broke into comical experiences and their most embarrassing moments, while Chuck paused only long enough to throw another volume on the fire. The last one dwindled into ashy embers while the sun rose and splashed a warm new day across their exhausted, toothy smiles.

Cowboy slowly rose, groaning under the exhaustion of the night and the morning's uncontrollable laughter. "There's just one more thing." He left the room and returned seconds later carrying his Stetson. "Might as well join the fun," he said dropping the hat on the burning heap. The flame burst back to life consuming it with a renewed appetite.

"Where do we go from here?" Chuck was holding his sore belly and rubbing the ache out of his smiling cheeks.

"I'm not sure," Cowboy gave the priest a widening smile, "but I can't wait to get started."

~~The end...~~
Beginning

Printed in the USA
CPSIA information can be obtained
at www.ICGtesting.com
JSHW020220280624
65464JS00004B/162